DOLPHIN SUMMER

DOLPHIN SUMMER

MONICA EDWARDS

with illustrations by
GEOFFREY WHITTAM

THE CHILDREN'S BOOK CLUB
121 CHARING CROSS ROAD
LONDON, w. c. 2

AUTHOR'S NOTE

*Strange though the story of Tamzin's
Simo may seem, there is nothing in it
that has not at some time been true of
some dolphin, somewhere in the world.*

© MONICA EDWARDS, 1963
PRINTED IN GREAT BRITAIN
COLLINS CLEAR-TYPE PRESS: LONDON AND GLASGOW

Contents

CHAPTER I

The Running Wind

TAMZIN and Meryon stopped playing tennis on the vicarage lawn at the sound of galloping hoofs and whirring wheels. They knew what it was, but it was always worth watching, and together they rushed to the pebble-dashed garden wall and looked over. As they expected, round the corner of Smiling Morn the grocer's fence, there burst into sight Jim Decks's black racing-donkey and little painted fish-cart. Surmounting the cart in a cloud of white hair and beard and bouncing ear-rings was the ferryman himself.

Once, Tamzin had got him started with a fruit and vegetable round in a retired and painted-up hearse, because no one could live on the ferry takings nowadays. That hadn't lasted. Jim thought it an indignity in a seaman, and too humdrum. He never had learnt to drive *Emma* the hearse in any safety, and finally sold her cheaply to Meryon who had recently reached seventeen years and passed his driving test.

Before and after that there had been one or two more ideas, mostly rather dubious and all short-lived. Now Jim had sprung this idea of his own. Vegetables might be demeaning, but it was proper for a fisherman to sell fish. No one knew where he had bought the donkey, whom he called Skylark in the boating tradition. All that Jim would tell anyone was that he had been a real racing-donkey. Selling fish with Skylark was almost exciting enough even for a retired smuggler like old Jim. Their whirlwind progress through the village brought out customers with plates to gaze and marvel and stand ready for their return; some, even, who had professed never to eat fish at all. But lately the fish had been scarce in the bay, no one knew why.

"He's got a cargo," Tamzin said. "Oh, good! I didn't know any boats had been out since the gales." The vicar's daughter was three years younger than Meryon who was her special friend. She was fair as he was dark, and slight as he was tough. Standing ready to cheer them on with a waving racket, she was surprised when Skylark slid to a halt with a jingle of harness close under the wall. He stood pawing the ground like a little war-horse, rolling his eyes. Holding the reins taut, old Jim leaned from the cart in the rollicking summer wind and shouted: "Mackerel's in the bay! Boats is all going out."

"How d'you know?" Tamzin shouted back into the wind, her long hair blowing.

"Seagulls—there's a million seagulls out there, gal. You could see 'em from your front garden."

Tamzin glanced at Meryon. A great cloud of seagulls in July fetched fishermen as surely as the lifeboat gun brought out the crew; they both knew this.

"Coming fer crew, then, ole young 'uns?" Skylark was shaking his bridle, receiving messages of imminent departure down the reins, like a telephone call. "I lay I'll goo arter 'em in ole *Thunderer*."

Thunderer was the ferryman's veteran fishing-smack, whose crew were long since dead except for the skipper himself.

Another glance flashed. "Of course!"

"Pile in then, smartish. Us carsn't be last down the river."

"But I must just tell Mother!" Tamzin was half turned

to dash across the lawn. "Meryon'll help run the sails up till I get there. Don't go without me, whatever you do."

The whirlwind went back round the grocer's corner, dust clouding the wheels, as Tamzin rushed in at the vicarage back door. Over her shoulder she saw Meryon's broad back beside Jim on the driving seat, black hair and white hair flying in the wind. Meryon's notorious ancestor, the Sussex pirate Tonkin Fairbrass, might have approved of the looks of the last of the Fairbrasses, but would certainly have disapproved of his honest eye and intentions of becoming a doctor.

"Mother, darling! The mackerel are in the bay and the boats are going out. It's all right if we go with Jim, isn't it?" She stood swinging on the kitchen doorpost. "We'll come back dry and sound and hung with mackerel."

Mrs. Grey was hunting through the dresser drawer for two matching garden gloves. She wore her long brown hair in a plait that went round her head, and she was lightly built like Tamzin. Her usual expression was one of loving approval, which made her family and other people feel warm and wanted.

"Then you must help to souse them. Soused mackerel would be nice, and it's the only way to keep a quantity if you haven't a freezer. And you'd better take pullovers; it's always colder on the sea. Find one of Dad's for Meryon. Why are *all* the garden gloves always left-hand ones?"

Tamzin gave her mother a great hug. "Because you wear out all the right ones. You must learn to weed two-handed, Mamariti!" She was racing upstairs for the pullovers. Her father's old sailing guernsey would do for Meryon, who hadn't brought one. A wail from the open garden door came up to her ears.

"Oh, could I go, too? I've never gone after mackerel!"

It was her brother Diccon, who was nearly eight. She held her breath, listening as she rummaged in a drawer.

"Not until you can swim the whole length of the harbour, my son, from the ferry right to the old moorings."

Tamzin offered silent thanks, snatching up the navy-blue guernsey. Diccon was as hard to keep an eye on in a boat as a couple of pups. Leaping downstairs she heard her mother's voice with comfort in it. "If you catch Banner and saddle him, we'll go down the sea wall and watch them from the beach. We could take your shrimping net, and some tea."

Three smacks and five small fishing-boats went out of the river to the mackerel. They were nearly all that was left of Westling's once fine fishing fleet. Jim's battered old *Thunderer* was not the first, but she was not the last, either. Tamzin threw herself aboard and began at once to help cast off the warps. She and Meryon grinned with Jim when the old smack creaked out from her moorings and took the wind ahead of Walter Goddard's *Samphire*.

"What did you do with Skylark?" she asked Meryon as they coiled down ropes.

"There's always a horde of small boys and girls—mostly Lillycrops—around his stable on a Saturday."

She grinned again. "Yes, of course: and Butterbeans Pope."

"We just leapt out and left everything to them."

"Look at the seagulls! He was right about millions. What a pity it so often has to be a glut or a famine."

The ferryman watched the big mainsail from his place at the tiller, rubbing the ears of his ferry-cat Billingham, who always went to sea with him. "Thass right, all or nothen." He grumbled very loudly so that his voice would carry down the deck to them. He had very sharp ears, himself. "Mackerel don't never fetch nothen when they comes in a glut. Stands to reason. I knowed 'em forked on the fields fer manure, times. Other times folks is crying out fer 'em." His short pipe bobbed between his beard and white whiskers like a small boat in a rough sea.

Billingham stood on the taffrail and stared down at the swirling wake. Jim went on grumbling, though the summer day was exhilarating, with the lively wind full of sunshine and seagulls and little white clouds and flying spindrift. No one took any notice, not the cat nor Tamzin nor Meryon; they knew him, and that his moods were a part of him, variable as the winds and the weather. By the time the *Thunderer* was out of the river mouth, curtsying to the Channel waves, he had grumbled himself out. They were carrying jib and mizzen now, the red sails swelling in the wind. One smack, the Tomsetts' *Alice*, swept out ahead of them, turning into the wind towards the seagulls. One by one the others came dipping behind them, red sails and white sails and puttering little engines, like dancers coming on to a stage. The seagulls screamed and swooped and soared, weaving their complicated patterns in the air; scooping the whitebait that had brought the mackerel and riding the wind.

"I know what this wind is," Meryon remembered. "It's the beginning of the July Runners."

"Thass right, mate; thass the Running Wind. That always fetches the mackerel."

"So that's why all the boats were ready," Tamzin exclaimed. She was at the tiller now, she and the ferry-cat, while Jim and Meryon got ready the trawling gear. "You were looking for them."

"'Course we was, gal. I lay there ent a bloke in Westling what don't watch out fer the seagulls, come the July Runners. I lay you musta bin at school other years, time the mackerel was in the bay, or you'd a knowed, too."

Dazzled by the sun and the water-sparkle and the glint of white feathers, Tamzin suddenly saw something else.

"Jim, Meryon, look! Porpoises or something jumping!"

"Them's dolphins, gal, bottle-nosed dolphins. Channel fleas, we call 'em, account of they jump so high. The mackerel fetches 'em; they foller the shoals."

She said: "July brings the Runners, the Runners bring the whitebait, the whitebait bring the mackerel and the mackerel bring the dolphins;" but the others were too busy shooting the trawl to listen. "I've seen dolphins before, of course," she said, "but only odd ones, and I always thought they were porpoises. What's the difference?"

"Size, mostly," Meryon answered, paying out rope. "Dolphins can be ten or twelve feet long, bigger than porpoises; and they have snouts instead of blunt noses."

"Keep yer course steady!" Jim shouted to her, and presently came pounding down the deck to take the tiller himself. Tamzin was glad to be able to lean on the gunwale and stare entranced at the gulls and the leaping dolphins and the dark shadow on the sea that was the packed multitudes of the mackerel.

"Git in the way of the fishing, they do, them dolphins," grumbled Jim. "Eat enough to sink a battleship, too."

Tamzin gazed at them, thrilled with the beauty and exuberance of their joyful leaping. They came rollicking out of the waves to windward; it was impossible not to believe that they were coming to look more closely at the fishing-boats, out of downright curiosity.

"They're the lads fer racing with the wind," Jim said, and the *Thunderer* ploughed on to meet them, dragging her wide nets.

"It isn't the wind, they're coming to us!" Tamzin cried.

"It wouldn't be the first time," said Meryon, "from all

the legends there are about them. We learned one when we were doing Herodotus, about the poet and singer, Arion. How he was made to jump overboard by pirates, but a dolphin came and took him to land on its back."

"That's just what it is, then! They know there's a pirate's descendant on board." Her eyes sparkled.

"Waiting for me to throw you in, I see."

Now the boats were running right into the shoal. The mackerel were so thick that they jostled up out of the water, and the gulls dive-bombed them in thousands. Leaning over, Tamzin saw the bow cleaving through birds and fishes. The noise of the seagulls clamoured round her ears. Then suddenly the dolphins were jostling very close; so close that, if she could have reached down so far, she could have touched the nearest of them.

"Ar, thass a masterpiece, that is," said Jim, gloating over a sea alive with fishes.

"Sing your last song," Meryon said to Tamzin.

"Arion didn't have a retired smuggler to protect him from his pirates, you great thug."

"Just look at them," he said. "Perfectly adapted for living in the sea. You couldn't improve on that shape."

"Did you see?" she cried suddenly. "They're rubbing against the boat! Like—well, like cats, the way they rub your ankles. Look at them gazing at us! They seem more like people than fishes."

Meryon was leaning over watching them with as much interest as Tamzin, but his was a biologist's interest. "They *are* more like people than fishes. They aren't fishes at all; they're mammals, like us."

"Garn," said Jim disbelievingly. "And them with tails and fins."

Then suddenly there was a great flurry of work on deck, Jim shouting that they were through the shoal and going about. Orders barked out, hands hauled on sheets, booms swung over. It was tricky, with eight boats fishing the area, but Tamzin was more concerned about hitting the dolphins than colliding with others of the fleet.

"We can't hit them," Meryon reassured her. "Nobody could. They've got a sort of built-in sonar, like bats, in a way. They know where we are before they see us."

"How do you know?" She was often astonished at the things he knew.

"Oh, just reading the papers; that kind of thing."

When they were on course again and sailing back through the shoal old Jim took the tiller from Tamzin. "Was a dolphin in New Zealand, time I were a young 'un," he said, his eye on the *Alice* sailing close. "Pelorus Jack. Called him that account of he patrolled in Pelorus Sound. Used to pilot the steamers through; truth he did; did it for more'n twenty years. I see him, meself, three-fower times."

Meryon was listening reflectively, a little reservedly; he was familiar with old Jim's tales. But Jim was telling a true one this time and Meryon's reserve annoyed him. He banged a hairy hand down on the tiller. "I tellee it's gospel! Use ter rub hisself agen the ship's side, he did, and ride in the bow-wave, and he were faster nor any steamer what sailed. Say there was two steamers going through the Sound, he'd pilot the fastest. People went from all over the world to see Jack. Ar, that were a rum do, were that."

Tamzin was watching the leaping dolphins, especially one which dived repeatedly under the keel just as Pelorus Jack probably had done. She had a wild half-hope that it would stay with them, but in a minute it streaked away and was racing with the five small fishing-boats across the Running Wind.

Jim's mind was on his nets which were pulling heavily

now, but he finished his tale. " He were the only fish what ever had a Order in Council signed fer him."

Meryon let it pass. Why shouldn't Jim call a mammal a fish if he wanted to? Jim knew more about dolphins than Tamzin or he would ever know.

"Which was," said Jim, "as no one were to catch any dolphin in or near Cook's Strait, or be fined as much as a hunnerd pound, a lot of money in them days. But it were Pelorus Jack they was thinking of, not any other dolphins." The old man leapt to his feet. "Take the helum, now, gal; I lay the nets is fair busting wi' fish. Come on, me lad, hands to the winch!"

CHAPTER II

A Sousing of Mackerel

WHEN Tamzin and Meryon came back that evening, hung with mackerel as she had prophesied, they found Roger and Rissa at the vicarage. These two were cousins, both a little older than Tamzin. Roger's home was on the farther side of Winklesea, the ancient small town where Meryon lived, a couple of miles from Westling over the Marsh. Rissa lived at Dunsford, an even older town about the same distance away, the two towns making a triangle with Tamzin's village. These four young people had been friends for so long, now, that even Tamzin's special link with Meryon had not divided them.

Rissa and Roger were furious at having missed the fishing.

"We were here only half an hour or so after the boats went out. We watched them sail out of the river." Rissa impatiently pushed back her short dark hair that was cut like a boy's.

"What a shame. We didn't know you were coming," Tamzin said. "You can take back lots of mackerel anyway."

"Fishing good?" asked Roger. In complete contrast to Meryon he was an ordinary looking boy with straight mousy hair and none of Meryon's natural flamboyance. The one thing he did have that others sometimes envied was a cheerful temperament that wasn't readily disturbed. He was easy to get on with. People liked him. This was really because he was so interested in nearly everyone, but the others seldom realised it and thought he must have some particular and mysterious charm, not seen on the surface as Meryon's was.

"Imagine a sea stiff with fish as a plum-cake mixture with raisins," Meryon said, "and you have it. Where shall we put the mackerel?"

Mrs. Grey came in with an armful of newspapers from the store-cupboard. "Pile them on the table," she said, spreading the papers. "We can all get round it to clean them."

The scrubbed pine table stood under the open window. Orange-tawny curtains, which Mrs. Grey had chosen to match the orange-tawny weather-tiles on the outside walls, were fluttering to the July Runners. A great white dresser stood against one wall. It was crowded with all the vicarage china; blue tea-service and a glorious dinner-service with many-coloured Chinese pheasants. A jumble of knife-box, letters, books, and piled-up wooden fruit-bowl was on the lowest shelf.

"We need cleaning, too," Meryon said cheerfully; "but that'll wait. While the kitchen's full of fish no one will know if it's us or them that's smelling."

"I wouldn't mind smelling for a week to have gone after mackerel with Jim," Rissa stated.

Tamzin was dumping the strings of fish that hung round her neck like a kind of sea-goddess's garland. "My hair's in a state," she said; then, "Why didn't you phone, or something?"

"Do we ever? You know we often come down on a Saturday."

"Nothing would have held back Jim for half a moment," Meryon said, wiping his hands on his trousers, which were old and slightly baggy.

"But, oh, I do wish you had seen the dolphins," Tamzin said. "They were the best thing."

A sound of clattering hoofs and whirring wheels brought everyone's eyes to the window, as the sound of Jim's bull-roarer fog-horn would bring the customers hurrying to their doors.

"It just can't be him," said Tamzin, gazing at him for the brief second of visibility; "he was still on board only fifteen minutes ago."

"He's like the old fire-engines," Roger said. "Three minutes from call to departure. It's so that he'll be in time to sell a nice load for people's suppers."

Smelling fish from the garden in some miraculous way, the two vicarage cats, Willow and Schnooky, came bounding in. Tamzin gave them some fish-heads in saucers. A mingled growling and crunching noise accompanied the fish-cleaners' work. Both the cats were short-haired; Willow was as grey and sleek as pussy-willow catkins before they open, and Schnooky was a sandy-ginger son of the sailing ferry-cat. They preferred plaice but mackerel was obviously all right.

In the middle of all this Diccon came rushing in. It was past his bed-time but Mrs. Grey didn't bother greatly on Saturdays, as long as her family were clean and tidy in time for church the next morning. "Butterbeans and I have been playing at fire-engines!" he said, as if he had heard Roger's remark. "We got all Skylark's harness ready, and roped it up over his back in the stable, the ropes going over the rafters, you know."

"Wash those black hands before you touch the fish, my son."

Diccon put them behind his back. "And then we pulled the cart up near the door, and went to stand lookout on the jetty."

"I think that was a waste of effort." Rissa dumped another fish-head on the pile in the middle of the table. "You could see the sails from nearly anywhere."

Diccon ignored her. "And then as soon as *Thunderer* came into the harbour we sounded the alarm and rushed to lower the harness on to Skylark's back, the way the old firemen did; and by the time Jim came along he only had to plonk the fish-boxes in the cart and jump up and go. Can I do some gutting with my new knife if I do wash my hands?"

"I hope you remembered to take the ropes off the harness?" Tamzin felt a little apprehensive, thinking of Skylark tripping himself up, but Diccon only answered with a reproving look.

"If you give the cats any more they'll be sick," said Mrs. Grey, seeing Roger glance at the empty saucers; but the cats felt the same about it and went slowly back to the garden again; there was no bouncing now.

Although it had seemed as if they never would be, all the mackerel were finally cleaned and washed. Some were set aside for Rissa and the boys, and the rest immersed in their dishes of spiced vinegar.

Tamzin and Meryon looked down at their fishy clothes and hands and sniffed loudly. "Well, anything that still smells now must be us," Meryon said.

"Baths," said Mrs. Grey. "And clean clothes, I do think; if you don't mind wearing the vicar's, Meryon?"

"I've worn his sailing togs so often, I've hardly the nerve to wear them again."

"Take them or leave them," came the vicar's voice from the hall; "you aren't going to have my clericals. Do I smell a cooking of soused?"

"You do indeed," said his wife.

"We'll toss up for the first bath," Tamzin said. "Oh, bother, I suppose Dicky's got to have it, now it's so late."

"I don't mind waiting; really I'd *like* to wait," said Diccon trying to sound unselfish, but his mother decided he could go to bed without a bath for once.

Meryon was rolling up fishy newspapers and making a parcel of the heads and tails and insides. "I lay baths is sissy, mates," he said in the ferryman's rich accents. "Reckon I'll go fer a hose-down out in the stable-yard. Where do I put these evidences of our crime?" he added in his own voice.

"Between the roses," said the vicar. "The soil's so poor; all shingle."

Roger was exclaiming with enthusiasm; "Oh, yes! I'll do the hosing! Clothes and all. Then you can just peg them out."

Rissa and Tamzin were carrying on a lively exchange of plans in a peaceful corner.

"If you phoned your mother now—or I will, if you like—I'm sure she'd let you stay the night. Then we could ride down to the beach before bed and see if we could see the dolphins. I don't mind riding Banner for once, as I'm smaller than you, and you can have Cascade."

Rissa's dark eyes widened as she considered the possibilities. She enjoyed riding Tamzin's half-Arab pony, a sensitive and beautiful grey, but her love was for her own chestnut mare. Siani was too wild ever to be really responsive as Cascade was, but something in Rissa's own rebellious nature responded to wildness in other creatures. She said: "Isn't it maddening not being able to keep my pony nearer! Castle Farm is perfect except for being in the middle of the Marsh." An idea suddenly fell into her mind. "It wouldn't take me long to ride out there on Cascade and bring Siani back. While you bath. She could stay in your paddock till to-morrow."

"It'll be dark by the time we get started."

They thought of the next thing nearly together. "Riding by moonlight is the best thing of all."

"Is there a moon?"

"Meryon, is there a moon?"

"He's planting fish-heads in the rose-bed," the vicar said. "But I can tell you; there's a half-moon. I thought you young people kept up with all the moon and tide phases."

"We do, in the holidays."

"If you're going to phone, I'll dash straight off, now," Rissa said.

"Don't gallop him too much!"

"As if I would."

"Ought someone to be looking at the soused?" the vicar asked; but no one answered. The kitchen was empty now except for two bulging cats. Upstairs the bath taps were running and Tamzin was banging about in the attic finding clothes in her chest of drawers. Diccon's laughter meant that his mother was reading his favourite book to him. Shouts from the stable-yard called Meryon to his hosing. A blast from the bull-roarer fog-horn, far down the street, called villagers to come for their suppers. A few minutes later the sound of hoofs in the stable-yard caused the vicar to look out of the scullery window. He was not in time to see Rissa's departure on Cascade, but he did greatly enjoy the sight of Meryon being hosed down like a dusty car on the cobbles. It was pretty obvious that the boys were enjoying it, too; and also that Tamzin was, judging from the glances up to the attic window. The vicar stood there grinning to himself, and suddenly laughed aloud.

CHAPTER III

The Moon Bathers

THE MACKEREL supper had been eaten and cleared away. Meryon's hearse, that had been old Jim's *Emma*, crunched down the vicarage drive in the settling dusk. Inside it as well as Meryon were Roger's bicycle and Roger, two large parcels of mackerel and Meryon's clothes still wet from the hosing. The headlights and the engine-noise passed down the village, and the vicarage sank back into the dusky silence of its garden. Light from a window flooded on to the vicar's roses and one great honey-drunk bee. For a minute or two there was no sound but the drowsy bumbling in the petals and the faraway murmur of the sea; nothing to see but stars and half-moon, a tall black chimney and the lighted roses.

Then there was low laughter in the stable-yard—because Diccon was asleep—and hoofs on cobbles. When she heard horse-shoes on the shingle drive Mrs. Grey glanced up from her letter-writing to the window, a little uneasy in her mind about the moonlight ride. The grey and the chestnut came into the light and passed out of it again, their riders waving.

"They'll be all right, my dear." The vicar divined her uneasiness.

"Perhaps I oughtn't to have said they could bathe."

Mr. Grey stretched out his legs, careful of Willow on his lap. "They're swimmers, and fairly sensible. It doesn't do to protect them too much."

Straining her ears to follow the ponies' steps, she heard the benighted bumble-bee and leaned out to rescue it. "I'll let it go in the morning, but they get so cold, poor greedy things."

Rissa and Tamzin rode out past the martello tower and on to the old sea wall that was a long green snake across the marshes to the sea. Tamzin had a moment of unreasonable fear, passing close under the high wall of the tower. It had always seemed to her sinister in the dark, huddled behind its shingle banks, crouching in its moat. Rissa didn't think about the tower at all, but only of the high thrill of night riding.

"All the Marsh to ourselves," she said with satisfaction.

"Except for the sheep. I do wish they wouldn't go to sleep in the middle of the path and then leap up so frantically."

"You've got nothing to complain of," said Rissa, whose pony had been shocked into circling in sudden panic. It was not so easy to control her without a saddle, but bareback riding fitted the mood of the evening, and Rissa loved a battle.

They cut corners of the twisting sea wall, cantering across the close-grazed levels. Siani in the moonlight was a swift dark shape like a horse's shadow. More white than grey, Cascade was like a wave, white-crested, smoke-tailed, a runaway from the white horses of the sea. Tamzin never grew out of pretending. She imagined she was surfing on a rush of spray; then she was riding on a dolphin's back like the poet Arion; then Cascade gave a great sneezing snort and was her own loved pony again.

Rissa always imagined she was riding a ferocious stallion, such as the battle-horse of Job who swallowed the ground in fierceness and rage and whose neck was clothed in thunder: or maybe Gramimund, Sorel or Marmorie, horses in the *Song of Roland* who went to war and were faster than swallows and falcons. It was easy to imagine these things with Siani.

The sea wall ran right from the grazings on to the beach banks of the shore. The ponies muscled into the loose surface like Arab horses into sand, heads down, shoulders thrusting. The net-sheds stood up black against the stars and sea. A moon-path ran out on the water like a road to France.

Tamzin said, "The only net-shed that has two good hooks on the wall, for tying the ponies, is the farthest one away towards the river. I think they used them for drying nets when they used to do keddle-net fishing off the shore."

Rissa jumped off Siani's back when they reached the shed. "Now the wind's dropped it's warm enough to undress on the beach, though the shed is open. There's nobody for miles." She tested the strength of the wall-hooks. The ponies wore halters under their bridles for easy tying. When they were undressing Tamzin kept thinking she could see the dolphins.

"I think it's only waves," Rissa said, pulling her jersey over her head; "the way they look in the moonlight."

"The ponies are staring out, too. I was imagining Cascade was a sea-horse," Tamzin added, a little apologetically, knowing Rissa's realistic mind but not knowing about the war-horses. "Perhaps he's longing to get back. But I don't think we'd see any dolphins if we went in on the ponies. Heavens, you have been quick. My hair takes so long to shove into a cap."

Rissa's was too short to bother with a cap. She piled her jeans and jersey on to a rucksack that bulged with their towels. "The tide could be higher, but never mind. Are you ready?"

"My feet are never really hard until the summer holidays," Tamzin said, walking tenderly on the stones.

The waves came in dark and curling, their crests crumbling into spray: like Cascade's mane, Tamzin thought. Wading in, their eyes scanned the dark shining bay. The water rose and fell in little black and silver humps. "It could be dolphins," Tamzin said.

"It could be waves."

Both were right.

"Perhaps if we swim out farther." The water was surprisingly warm.

"It always is when the air is cold; it's the contrast," Rissa said. She dived through a wave and came up shining with moon and water. Tamzin kept herself under the warm sea. They swam on slowly down the moon-path. Seagulls sleeping on the surface bobbed like toy ducks in a bath. They flew up with scatters of phosphorescence when the swimmers drew near.

"I could go on and on," said Tamzin, elated, "right to France."

"We've come out quite a way, already." Rissa felt responsible, as the elder. "Never mind about the dolphins." Tamzin was disappointed, she knew. Dolphins had caught her imagination. She would be writing poetry about them next. Rissa recognised the symptoms; the look of restlessness, as if she were listening for something, and a kind of wonder in her voice when she spoke about them.

It was too deep to touch the bottom where they were. They rolled over and floated for a while, more tired than they had thought. The sea was ruffled after the day's wind, so that swimming needed more effort. Tamzin shut her eyes and tried to frighten herself for the thrill of it, and Rissa stared at the sky trying to pick out constellations.

"Well, I know the Great Bear, anyway. And that little lot is Pleiades. How many in Pleiades can you count? You're supposed to have very good eyes if you can see more than seven. I say!" she said more loudly, as Tamzin didn't answer, "I hope the ponies are all right. Perhaps we ought to be getting back." There was still no answer. Rissa rolled over, treading water as she looked around her. "Tamzin!" A sudden cold fear began to settle somewhere in her chest. "Tamzin!"

A small shatter of seagulls went up, and that was all; except that, ironically, dolphins were now leaping, moon-shiny, near the river mouth. They must be dolphins, the dolphins that Tamzin had wanted her to see. They meant nothing to her now.

Rissa was not prone to panic. No one could have said she had a runaway imagination. But now, as never before in her life, she was gripped by a growing horror. What had happened? What to do? As she swam in small circles, shouting, her sensible brain tried to find an ordinary solution. Perhaps Tamzin had swum back quietly to the beach, just for the fun of it? But Tamzin was not like that. She was swimming under water, and so couldn't hear Rissa calling? But not for all this time. She was still close by, floating, and just not answering? No, that wouldn't do, either. There was no ordinary solution.

Tiring now, Rissa began making her circles closer to the shore, shouting, shouting, while she had breath. Her feet touched down on sand and she stood a moment panting, the hard breaths rasping in her throat. She could see the ponies standing against the sky. Tamzin was not there. Rissa shouted again, straining her eyes over the dark sea. Slowly, shivering with cold and horror, she began to face the stark probability that Tamzin had drowned. Get the ponies and gallop back for help, one half of her mind told her. No, stay and keep looking for her, the other half said. Hesitating, wading shorewards and looking back, Rissa suddenly noticed the dolphins. They were very close and coming closer from her left, two together and others at a distance. Their curved fins rode the water like little black sails. Some, leaping, scattered phosphorescence.

Then Rissa stared at the first two dolphins. She absolutely didn't believe what she was seeing, but a great surge of hope came over the disbelief. Between the flanks of the dolphins and supported by them was something not a dolphin. Waiting, she knew against all reason and common sense that it was Tamzin and that the dolphins were helping her. Rissa stood still in the water, afraid that any movement might frighten them away. Tamzin was clutching at the fin of one, but seeming scarcely conscious. The dolphins passed near to Rissa in the shallow water, letting Tamzin go as they slid under and away. Tamzin, too, would have slid under if Rissa had not jumped to catch her.

Somehow she got her to the beach. Tamzin was heavy and wet and limp; her feet made fumbling efforts to walk. Rissa was strong and fairly tough, but exhausted from swimming and shouting and anxiety. She pulled Tamzin's arm round her neck and got her a few steps farther up the shore. For some time she didn't give another thought to the dolphins; the whole thing was too mind-boggling.

Water in the lungs and stomach, she said to herself, always basically practical. The sloping beach would be just right. When they were safe from the sea she lowered Tamzin on to the shingle, turning her face-downwards with her head lower than her feet. Making sure that she could breathe freely, she turned her face sideways and scooped away the pebbles. Tamzin moved her hands, and water ran from the corner of her mouth.

Kneeling, Rissa pressed on Tamzin's back, tentatively and gently at first, in time to her breathing. More water trickled. She said, "You're all right, now! I'll look after you. Everything will be all right."

Suddenly she thought about warmth, and how important it was. "I'm just going to get clothes and towels; I shan't be a minute," she said, and turned to race up the beach bank to the net-shed. The ponies had been dozing. There was nothing for them to do, no hay to eat, and time hung heavily in the dark. Siani threw up her head as Rissa came running and what she saw was a black figure rushing towards her against the moon.

For a moment there was a wild rearing and snorting then Siani's halter broke and she was gone. Rissa reached out for Cascade who was pulling backwards. There was no time to think of Siani, nor even to glance as she galloped away into the mist that was rising from the Marsh; but life might depend on keeping Cascade. He jerked his head twice, looking at her wild-eyed. She talked to him softly, thinking all the time of Tamzin lying cold on the beach; but they must keep Cascade if she was to get Tamzin home in time. Time might be short if there was water in her lungs.

Cascade was a wise little horse and very gentle. Rissa felt him grow quiet under her hands. Quickly and as steadily as she could she took him and tied him to the door-latch at the front of the shed, where he couldn't look towards the Marsh. Then she gathered up the towels and all their clothes and ran back down the beach.

Tamzin was half-sitting, leaning on her hands. She had been sick. Rissa threw the towels round her, lifting and dragging her to a dry place. "Oh, I'm so glad you're all right!" She was rubbing with the towels, trying to bring warmth. "I'll look after you," she comforted. She was astonished, herself, to find such wells of comfort in her matter-of-fact nature. Now, nothing could express what she felt at Tamzin's just being alive, and not drowned and gone from them all for ever.

Tamzin said weakly: "Siani's gone."

"Yes, but it doesn't matter, we've got Cascade. You'll be home quite soon. Are you warmer? Do you feel better?"

Tamzin nodded. Having dried her, Rissa began dressing her as if she were smaller than Diccon. The jeans were the only difficult thing, because Tamzin was so limp. She pulled both the jerseys on, her own and Tamzin's; she was no longer cold herself, because of so much activity. Then, kneeling to rub Tamzin's hands she looked at her with anxious care. "Better?"

Tamzin nodded again. "I've got your jersey on."

"Oh, that's all right, I'm boiling; and I've got my jeans and the towels." She hesitated before bringing herself to mention the unbelievable thing in her mind. "The dolphins—they saved you." Perhaps Tamzin didn't realise.

"I know. Like Arion."

"Like what?" Rissa hadn't heard about Arion.

"Someone in a story."

"Oh." She wanted to know more of what had happened to Tamzin; someone in a story didn't matter. But there were more urgent things. "Could you get on Cascade if I bring him down? With me helping."

"I think so. I'm all right. Just a bit wobbly." She tested her legs while Rissa rushed back to the shed, but sat down again rather quickly.

It was difficult mounting Cascade. Tamzin could hardly believe that she often did it in one flying leap.

"If only we could get him to kneel, like a camel!" Rissa exclaimed. She was always full of ideas for training horses and dogs, and even cows. Finally she got Tamzin to a high ridge of shingle and brought Cascade below it, and then with a hand under Tamzin's knee hoisted her up.

"I'm sorry about Siani," Tamzin said, hunched over the saddle-tree as Rissa led the pony over the shingle.

"Someone will find her."

Hoofs and sandals fell silent as the beach banks merged with the Marsh. Siani was out there somewhere, on those mysterious night-wrapped grazings. Rissa gave her mind to more immediate things as she led Cascade homewards. The solemnity of what might have happened sobered them both.

"I thought you were dead."

"I thought I was going to be."

Neither of them felt like talking about it, then. Rissa strode on, caped in the towels and rucksack, leading the mist-coloured pony through the moonlit mist.

CHAPTER IV

Return to Life

AFTER the first shock of their arrival at the vicarage Mrs. Grey smothered her anxiety in the needs of the moment. No more questions were asked and Tamzin was not allowed to start explaining until she was wrapped in thick blankets, with hot-water bottles, in an arm-chair in the sitting-room. Rissa had already given a brief account of the little she knew, before turning out Cascade in the paddock.

Mr. Grey rubbed Tamzin's feet while her mother made hot drinks. Rissa came back indoors full of remorse. "We oughtn't to have gone out so far. I nearly lost Tamzin and now I may have lost Siani too. It was all my fault because I'm older."

"Then you're the only one who thinks so. It was both your faults: and you did as much as any human could, afterwards," Mrs. Grey told her. "I'm sure Siani will be all right; perhaps she's gone back to Castle Farm. Now, you can carry the tray in for me, if you like."

The hot drinks were very comforting. Rissa was wearing a spare pullover of Tamzin's, now. Watching her daughter with anxious eyes, Mrs. Grey decided not to fetch the doctor out from Dunsford at this late hour; there could be no water left in Tamzin's lungs when she looked so well and breathed so naturally.

"Now you can tell us what happened," she said when Tamzin's cup was empty and Rissa had taken it from her.

"Cramp after the mackerel supper? Though that was an hour earlier, at least."

"I don't really know what happened." Tamzin looked puzzled. "We were floating, as Rissa said. The water wasn't cold, and I didn't have cramp or anything. I just suddenly found I was slipping under. It was so quick, when I tried to shout I gulped water, and that made it difficult for me to get back."

"Could it have been an undercurrent?" Mrs. Grey looked at her husband.

"There is a current that sweeps downwards, towards the river mouth. It changes its run from time to time, Jim says, but I shouldn't have thought as far west as the sea wall."

Tamzin felt guilty. "We went in much nearer the river than usual. I suggested it, because the farthest net-shed has two hooks on the wall."

"Then it is possible. I've never heard of it happening to anyone else, but you might have been pulled into the current."

"And not Rissa?"

"Not if she were just clear of it. Currents are often clearly defined, like the warm and cold patches."

"I suppose the dolphins couldn't have pulled you down?" Rissa asked.

"It was the dolphins that saved me."

"Two of them. Lots of dolphins were in the bay."

"There was nothing near me at all. I just seemed to slide down, like sliding down a chute, and I couldn't swim up again. I thought I was drowning. Then something came under me, pushing. I thought, 'I'm being rescued,' but I was too hazy to think much. I didn't know then it was the dolphins."

Mr. Grey was listening closely, as if considering every word.

Rissa said, "It still seems incredible to me. I don't think I'd ever really have believed it if I hadn't seen it. In fact I hardly did believe it, when I saw them coming in." She reached for Schnooky who had jumped on to Tamzin's blanketed knee.

"You can leave him," Tamzin said. "I like to have him, and I'm perfectly all right, now."

The vicar said, "You know, it could have been quite normal dolphin behaviour."

"You mean, like their rescuing Arion? Meryon told me about that."

"I mean, because they do support each other in the water, when the need arises. Dolphins in large tanks have been seen doing it. They have to come to the surface to breathe, of course, and if one is sick or wounded the others help it up. Sometimes a mother pushes her new-born baby up. If a dolphin couldn't breathe it would drown."

"Perhaps they thought you were another dolphin," Tamzin's mother suggested.

The vicar shook his head. "I don't think so. Some people hold that dolphins are next in intelligence to man, of all the animals. They have huge complicated brains. You don't need much brain to know your own species."

"Besides, they brought her to *me*," said Rissa, marvelling as the thought struck her; "another of the same species."

"They could have been just taking her to the shore," the vicar said, "but even that shows reasoning. They wouldn't have taken another dolphin to the shore."

Tamzin was thinking back into the mixed horror and wonder of that moonlight bathe. "Really, it was one dolphin in particular, the one I held on to. The other came afterwards. Almost as if the first one had called it. I don't think any of the rest came anywhere near."

The vicar said, "There are a great many stories in the classics about dolphins rescuing and befriending humans; and there are old coins showing boys riding on dolphins."

"And dishes and cups the same," said his wife, who had seen prints of them. "And then for hundreds of years men and dolphins seem to have lost interest in each other."

"You know why I think that is?" the vicar said. "I think that ever since men learned how to make bigger ships, standing higher in the water, they lost touch with the dolphins and other sea animals. The little ships of earlier times brought them close enough to look each other in the eye."

In the morning, fairly early, Skylark and the fish-cart came whirling down the vicarage drive. Old Jim tied the donkey to the rose pergola and knocked on the front door, which already stood open to the early sunshine.

Tamzin was being kept in bed for breakfast, to her annoyance, but Rissa was just coming in from looking at Banner and Cascade and filling up their water tank. The vicar was at early service, Diccon was hunting for wood-lice under the tamarisks, and Mrs. Grey making coffee in the kitchen.

The ferryman encountered Rissa at the corner of the house. "Eh, gal, leastways you are on yer pins."

Rissa looked down at them, puzzled. "Oh, yes. Why?"

"Was you riding that fire-eating horse of yourn, or Tamzin? Eh, scupper me if I didden think one on you was likely dead or wownded."

"Oh, Siani! Have you found her? I've been awfully worried."

Diccon's face appeared in the middle of the tamarisks. "It was Tamzin it happened to, and she's still in bed. Could I get in the cart and turn it round when you want to go, Jim, please?"

Jim looked at Rissa appealingly. He had a very soft spot for Tamzin, who often annoyed him to the point of shouting at her.

"She's all right, really," Rissa told him, stroking Skylark's long ears.

There was the sound of a sash-window sliding up with a rush and a bang, and Tamzin leaned out as the others gazed up. "I'm getting up as soon as I've eaten something. Just so that Mother can feel I've had breakfast in bed."

"Eh, bless us, gal! Me and Jimmy and 'Stacia we wasn't half worried time we heard about that pony. I says I gooin' straight round, and 'Stacia she says take the gal some dabs fer her breakfast, case she's all right, see, and they're in me cart."

"Did she really?" Tamazin could hardly believe this of 'Stacia Decks, and was immediately sorry for all the unkind feelings she had had about her. "How kind! I'll have them, even if it means staying in bed later for them."

"You aren't in bed now," Diccon remarked.

Rissa looked at Jim anxiously through Skylark's ears. "Siani—d'you know where she is?"

"Castle Farm, ole young 'un. Bolted right back there, by the seem of it. She throw you orf, then?"

"Of course not." Rissa was indignant, though she had suffered this fate from Siani several times. "How did you hear about her?"

"We-ell, gal, I takes young Johnny Beatup over the ferry this morning early fer caddying at the links, and he say he had it orf Bob Smeed what lives on the Marsh and was gooin' shrimping, and he had it orf of Shepherd Tewmell what works fer Castle Farm as you do know."

"Well, thank goodness for that, anyway. She could have been half-way across the county by now."

"If somebody doesn't take the dabs in," Tamzin called, "I'll be bedridden all day."

Before Diccon had finished turning Skylark round, the *Emma* drew up at the drive gates with Meryon at the wheel. Old Jim rushed forwards, his hand raised like a traffic policeman. "One thing Skylark can't abide is motors. He fair savages 'em," he explained to Rissa.

Diccon took advantage of all this by going on driving Skylark, though with Jim at the bridle, up the drive and out past Meryon, who sat watching and grinning in his hearse, unsuspecting of any peril. At Smiling Morn the grocer's corner the ferryman jumped in too, and the fish-cart spanked off round the high fence with the two of them.

"That's a car-eating donkey, that is," Rissa told Meryon as the hearse slid elegantly down to the front door.

"Must be why he got him so cheaply." Meryon pulled on the hand-brake and pocketed the ignition key so that Diccon shouldn't be tempted. "Tamzin around?"

"In bed."

"What?"

"I'm not!" Tamzin called from the attic window.

"Well, you ought to be, Juliet," said Rissa. "I'm going to help fry dabs, and then I'm going out to see if Siani's all right."

Meryon looked up at Tamzin. His first thought was that she was beautiful, with her hair hanging over one shoulder and the sill; his next that something must be wrong, for her to be there on a golden July morning when everyone else was up and doing. "What's happened? Something has."

"Yes. But really I'm all right now. And I think you're too logical a biologist to believe what happened at all."

He looked at her for a minute. "I'm coming up."

"Bring my breakfast, then! I'm being kept in bed for it, of all things."

In the end nearly everyone took breakfast up to Tamzin's room under the roof, where the ceiling came down like the sides of a tent. Tamzin's bed with its patchwork cover was between north and south windows so that if she looked to the left she could see the river and the sea; if to the right, the village stretching away to her father's little church, and, beyond that, red-roofed Dunsford on its hill. Tamzin had only one chair, but nobody minded, finding places on the foot of her bed or even on the floor on her red Turkey rug, balancing plates on their knees. Only Diccon was absent, not having returned from Jim's, but Mrs. Grey was not worried. "'Stacia will give him just the same as we're having. She's really much kinder at heart than she seems."

Everyone was rather gay that morning. It was because Tamzin was obviously perfectly well and unharmed by her desperate experience. Only Meryon saw it differently, and was quieter than usual. Ever since he and Tamzin had formed their special friendship he had told himself that one day he might lose her, perhaps to someone more worthy; but he had not thought of the possibility of losing her by death. It was very sobering. When you were young you could easily imagine things going on the same nearly for ever, but really you knew that they could come to an end in a single night. Last night, for him, the most important thing had nearly ended.

Tamzin was talking about the dolphins. She wanted to go straight out to the beach and see if they were there. She felt that, in a way, she owed it to them.

"But you can't *thank* them," Rissa said reasonably; "and you can't really give them anything, or even do anything for them."

"I know. But I think I ought to go, all the same. Just

going there is a kind of thanks. It's all I can do, anyway."

"No swimming to-day, however well you feel," her mother said firmly. "One day of going carefully, and then back to normal to-morrow."

"Oh, Mamariti!"

"We could sail round in Jimmy's *Kittiwake*," Meryon said, knowing how much it meant to her. "I don't expect Jimmy will be using her, and it's a good day for sailing, tide right and everything."

Tamzin's father smiled at her. "You can be like the early Greeks and Romans, getting to know your dolphins from a little boat." He looked at his watch. "Who's coming to church?"

"All of us, I expect," said Mrs. Grey, gathering up plates, "except Rissa, who wants to make sure Siani's all right."

"If any would care to trust themselves to it—and to me," said Meryon, "my horseless carriage is at the door."

CHAPTER V

No Formula for This

OLD JIM'S Jimmy was out in his smack, *Stormy Petrel*, following the mackerel down the coast as were most of Westling's fishermen. Jim himself had gone with him, closing the ferry for the day although it was a fine summer Sunday when customers were always fairly plentiful; for the mackerel would be much more profitable. Tamzin and Meryon took three boat-loads of passengers over the river before pushing off in *Kittiwake* themselves.

"By way of rental for borrowing the dinghy," Meryon said to Tamzin.

"And because people always look so pathetic standing waiting for things that don't come," said Tamzin, "whether it's buses or ferrymen or the end of the world."

When they were finally sailing down the river to the sea, with the Running Wind in their faces and white clouds overhead, Meryon looked at her and wished that he could find dolphins for her, or anything else she wanted. He said, "I can't help thinking your dolphins may have gone with the mackerel, too." She looked like a kind of golden figurehead, he thought, sitting in the bows with her tawny hair blowing and her tawny-golden skin. Her feet were bare and she wore her sleeves and the legs of her jeans rolled up. She looked so much alive, it was impossible to think of her as she might have been but for two dolphins.

For all her romanticism and high imagination, Tamzin had a way of accepting things without fuss. Things that could be fought, such as cruelty to an animal, she would fight; but things that were inevitable, such as dentists and the weather, she had learned to accept. "I know, I don't really expect to see them; or, even if we do, that they'll take any notice. But I just feel I owe it to them. Last night I couldn't even give them a grateful look, I was so far gone."

"It isn't only you that owes them something. Nor even only you and I."

Leaning as the dinghy leaned to the wind, she accepted this, too. Love of family and friends was a part of life. Not of everyone's life, but this was hard to imagine. She said, "You know how people sometimes have a kind of emblem, special to themselves; perhaps I mean a mascot? Well, I'm going to have dolphins."

"I'll carve you one," he said. "It's time I did some more wood-carving."

The run downstream to the sea was long and straight, and after a minute he added, "The jib will look after itself till we run into the bay."

Tamzin came down the dinghy and sat with him at the tiller. Neither of them spoke for a long time. The nice thing about Meryon, Tamzin thought contentedly, is the way you don't feel you must keep talking to him. Of all the things I like about Tamzin, Meryon thought, one of the best is that she doesn't natter.

Running out of the river into the bay she was back at the jib-sheet, both of them concerned only with sailing the dinghy. *Kittiwake* cantered over the breakers, Tamzin said, always deliberately mixing up her horses and boats. She screwed up her eyes to scan the whole wide ruffling bay in the sunlight; but there were no flashing clouds of seagulls, no mackerel, and no dolphins to be seen. On the horizon three small steamers trailed their scarves of smoke behind them, and off Fairlight an outboard motor-boat droned as it churned its white wake.

"You can't blame them," Tamzin said, suddenly realistic in almost a Rissa-ish way. "You can't expect even a dolphin to have noble thoughts on an empty stomach. Father was only saying in his sermon last week how even Jesus, who was very spiritual, always thought of feeding people."

"Which reminds me," said Meryon, delving in his pocket and pulling out a bar of nut chocolate. "Have a piece."

"Do you think," she said, peeling off silver-paper, "that if the mackerel were still in the bay my dolphins would have known me? That I was the human thing they rescued, I mean? Or do you think I was just any old sinking lump, and it was their instinct to heave it up?"

"If you're asking me if I think you were any old sinking lump——"

"I didn't; I said might they have thought so?"

"Impossible," he said. "No one could think so."

She gave up trying. "You're hopeless."

"I know; I'm a case," he said. "Had it coming on for years."

They sailed on nearly to Fairlight, hugging the shore. *Kittiwake* bounced in the motor-boat's wake; like a horse shying at a traction-engine, Tamzin said; and Meryon said lazily who could want to racket about with all that noise when there was sailing. He kept his gaze out on the bay, partly to look for the dolphins but as much because he didn't care to look at the place where Tamzin nearly drowned.

When they had gone about and were sailing back, Tamzin was resigned to disappointment. "Anyway, it's been a lovely sail."

"It still is a lovely sail."

"Everything seems especially and very sharply good, somehow, to-day: as if I'd been reprieved. Perhaps you can't ever know how good life is, unless you've nearly been dead."

Meryon said nothing, staring over the sparkle and dance of water. Tamzin looked out, too, over the bay. The sea slapped the *Kittiwake*'s sides and rustled foamily under her bows as she raced for home. The Running Wind drove flocks of clouds like sheep and ruffled the sea into little hurrying waves. Idly watching them, Tamzin rejected a sudden wild speculation when one far-distant wavelet seemed to move more swiftly than the rest. She looked away, to Meryon, but he was looking at the same far place. She said to herself: If it's still there when I look back . . . And it was, but nearer, much nearer. Her hands were on the *Kittiwake*'s side as she gazed, refusing to believe so improbable a thing: but last night's events had been more than improbable, and true.

Meryon turned the *Kittiwake* slowly into the wind slackening the mainsheet. At once Tamzin's hands went to the jib, but her eyes stayed on the little wave, as Meryon's did. Under the gaze of both of them the wave leapt clear of the water, and again, and again.

"Did you see that? Did you see?" Tamzin cried.

Meryon nodded. What could one say? The dinghy slowed, her sails slapping as she hove-to; and fast, faster than the motor-boat, the leaping came towards them.

"It's my dolphin! It must be my dolphin! The only one in all the bay that didn't follow the mackerel."

"It isn't the only one; look behind it."

Tamzin had had no eyes for anything else, but now she glanced quickly from the swift-approaching dolphin and saw another, less joyfully rollicking but following some fifty feet behind.

"Both my dolphins!" She sounded awed and incredulous now, her voice so quiet that Meryon hardly heard it. He kept the dinghy hove-to as the nearer dolphin came racing towards them, tentatively followed at a distance by the second. His biologist's mind did not know what to think; he had no formula for this. Tamzin didn't need a formula. She leaned on the dinghy's side, half kneeling, half sitting sideways, watching. The dolphin came so fast, mostly under the surface, that she thought it must hit them or dive, but suddenly it stopped. There was no disturbance of the water, though the stop had been instant. Meryon was so astonished by this that almost he felt they must both be dreaming the whole thing, since surely anything travelling in water at thirty miles an hour must cause turbulence at a sudden halt. Much later, when involvement with dolphins impelled him to read all he could find about them, he learned that this smooth halt at speed was typical of them and still a mystery to scientists.

Tamzin reached her hands down into the water. Meryon would hardly have been any more astonished, after the events of the past night and day, if the dolphin had come into them; but as if the boat had been its goal it rubbed along the planks, going under and up the other side, and playing round the bows as the dolphins had done around the fishing-smacks. The second dolphin came no nearer, but kept its distance, swimming under and over so that it looked like a big turning wheel.

Neither Tamzin nor Meryon remembered how long they were there, with the slack sails flapping and the dolphin playing round them. Once or twice Tamzin touched it as it slid past, but the dolphin was elusive. There was nothing to show that it was not simply the boat that attracted it, as a seal will play with a ball. Realising this, Tamzin felt ashamed of thinking that it had come because it knew her. Then suddenly, with a flip of its mermaid-tail, it turned and raced back the way it had come, the second dolphin in attendance as before. Both of them dived, and though Meryon and Tamzin watched the bay for some time there was no more sign of them.

She turned to Meryon, her eyes dazzled with sun on water. "Do you think they were my dolphins?"

"How can one say?" He knew she wanted to think it,

and he wished he could have said: Yes, of course they were; but honesty was natural to him, especially in things connected with science and life, and especially again when he was with Tamzin. "They played just like that with the fishing-boats."

"Yes, but that was when all the dolphins were there, and they were excited about the mackerel. These two stayed behind."

"After last night I'm beginning to think that almost anything is possible." He was pulling in the slack main-sheet. "But I'm also thinking that if we don't shiver some timbers now we'll miss the tide."

"If they're there to-morrow, just two dolphins, they would almost certainly be my two, wouldn't they?" She was busy at the jib, talking over her shoulder, watching the wind fill the sail.

"Will you be allowed to swim to-morrow?"

"Oh, surely: I'm going to school."

"Tide will be lowish, but I'll come straight over after school, shall I? I might bring Roger."

"What a blight school is! We could have gone down in the morning. Perhaps the dolphins will think we aren't coming, and go away."

He smiled at her, pushing over the tiller as the dinghy took the wind. "That might give you your answer!"

CHAPTER VI

Dolphin's Company

DASHING in from school on Monday Tamzin said she wouldn't have any tea because of swimming, but would save up for supper. Tea was in the garden because the July Runners had died down and the sun was warm.

"Have a glass of milk and an apple," her mother suggested, "just to keep you going. How's the day been? Are you sure you feel all right for a swim? Not tired or anything?" She looked up at Tamzin from her deck-chair with loving concern.

"No, I'm perfectly all right. Really I am."

Mrs. Grey wanted to say all kinds of anxious things such as: do be careful not to go out too far, won't you? and not to tire yourself; the idea of an undercurrent really does worry me; perhaps you oughtn't to go out of your depth there, at all. Instead she said, "Well, take care of yourself, lovey," knowing that Meryon, and probably Roger, would be with her, and that all of them were sensible and would be especially cautious after the near-disaster.

"I will, Mummy." She drank the milk, watching the cats racing up and down the damson tree.

"Oh, could I go, too?" Diccon pleaded. Always he seemed doomed to be left behind.

Tamzin said, "You've just eaten two great hunks of bread and honey; you'd sink like a stone. And you told

Butterbeans that you'd help him muck out Skylark's stable. I suppose there's nothing to stop you going out to the beach to watch, if you can get back by bedtime, but I don't expect there'll be anything to see." She took an apple from the bowl on the trolley. "I'll just say hallo to Cascade, Mamariti, and then go round to see if Jim's back. When Meryon comes will you tell him?" Roger and Meryon had to travel from school in Hastings and would be later than she was.

Cascade had the apple-core, except for a piece she gave to Banner to make things fair. She thought about Siani out at Castle Farm. Rissa had reported at school that morning that all was well, but that the Merrows at the farm had been worried enough to search the Marsh when they found the pony outside the orchard gate early in the morning. There was no telephone at the farm and they were some distance from a call-box.

Old Jim was back at the ferry when Tamzin went round. The mackerel had all been unloaded and sold at New-haven; there was nothing for Skylark's fish-cart, nor to stop the ferryman sticking out his feet and listening while Tamzin told about her dolphins. She was a little afraid that he would receive her story with scorn and disbelief, but Jim loved fishermen's tales, the wilder and more improbable the better. His reaction was always to try to cap them with still more incredible tales, and he began to do so as soon as he saw an opening. Now Tamzin listened, to whale tales and shark tales and dolphin tales, and she hugged the ferry-cat as she listened, sitting on the bench outside Jim's hut.

"Well, this dolphin what I was telling you I sewed up, we catched him in the net, he had a dang great hole in his side, see. I says to my mate, 'He been in someone's propeller,' I says, 'I lay I'll sew him up.' 'You wunt, then,' he say, 'they make wunnerful fine eating, I lay we eat him.' Come to blows, it did. I din arf belt him smartish, a proper rumbustion, that were."

"What about the dolphin when you were fighting?" she asked anxiously.

"They can live longer outen water, mate, nor what they can under, s'long as they don't git dry. A dolphin'll drown, kep' under water, they got to breathe, same as you and me. Well, there was a fair sea running, sloshing on the deck, so he were all right. Now when I done with the mate I gits me darning needle and thread, what I keep in the cabin, see, and set down and darns up the dolphin, same as if he were a pair of trowsis. He knowed as I were helping him, and never moved; but he looked at me outen his eye, just same as you might, gal. Got eyes like humans, nearly, they have."

"I know," said Tamzin.

"When I done darning him I brings the mate round with a bucket of water and says, ' Gimme a hand throwing of the dolphin over,' and he never offers no objection, so we puts him over. Next day we was fishing them waters again and scupper me if that dolphin didden come swooshing to the boat and start rubbing hisself alonger the side. I tellee true."

"But are you sure it was the same dolphin, Jim?" This was Tamzin's own problem.

"That were him, all right; I reckernized me handiwork. He come a dunnamany times that summer, but not to no one else's boat. I use ter lean over and scratch him with the ole boat-hook. He like that. Ar, that were a rum do, that were."

Tamzin wanted to ask if Jim thought it might have been the boat his dolphin came to, and not Jim himself. After all, it was ships that had appealed to Pelorus Jack when he piloted the steamers through the Sound, and there was the way they had played round the boats at the mackerel fishing. But the *Emma* was already coming round Smiling Morn's corner, with Meryon and Roger inside.

The sun was still warm and high when the three of them were walking down the sea wall. Trotting ahead on Banner and Skylark were Diccon and Butterbeans Pope. It seemed sad to Diccon that he must be home for eight o'clock bedtime, when Butterbeans had no bedtime at all; the longer he stayed out the better his family liked him. Generally he lived in Skylark's stable, taking his hunk of bread and butter or pie with him to be out of the way of his swarming small brothers and sisters. It suited Jim very well to have an unpaid stable-boy and this was how Butterbeans sometimes got a bareback ride, though Jim had no saddle for Skylark, and only short string reins tied to the blinker-bridle. Butterbeans would have been amazed to realise how Diccon envied his vagabond please-yourself life. To his way of thinking, Diccon simply lived in heaven, where people actually minded if you came in late, or were wet or hungry, or had toothache.

There was seldom anyone down at the beach on this side of the river, except sometimes shrimpers and longshore fishermen. This was because of the lack of a motor road, and the fact that when one had walked the mile down the sea wall there was no sand for tender feet except at low water. Sitting happily on the shingle pulling off their shoes, Tamzin and the boys could see the people like ants on the sands across the river.

"But no dolphins," said Roger, scanning the water. Not that he had really expected to see them, but he had been hoping. The sea was so calm, since the wind had dropped, that even a surfacing fin would have been seen at once.

Tamzin was still hoping. After the emergence yesterday of dolphins from a deserted sea, how was anyone ever to say where they were?

It was two hours to low water and the tide was already far out, exposing stretches of shining wet sand. Diccon and Butterbeans had cantered over it to splash pastern-deep along the sea's margin. Their hoof-prints, filling with water, made a double track down from the shingle to the sea. Tamzin pulled off her shirt and jeans under her big towel, as she and Rissa had done in the moonlight two days ago, but nothing else was the same.

Roger was saying, "Don't you *mind* going in again, so soon after what happened?" He was rather admiring her for it.

She said, pushing her hair into her cap; "No. But I shan't go in far."

"You certainly won't go far from *me*," said Meryon.

"All right, you big bully."

They ran down beside the donkey and pony tracks, adding their footprints. The small waves came to meet them, their ridges crumbling into foam. Tamzin wore an old blue swim-suit with her Bronze Medal badge sewn on it. Meryon had passed the Silver earlier that term, and now remembered it ironically. Little good it had been in the time of Tamzin's need, he reflected; and then remembered that Rissa and Roger too had taken their Bronzes when Tamzin had taken hers, and Rissa had been there. You can't do much to help anyone who vanishes as Tamzin had done; and Rissa had been magnificent when she was able to get going.

Five minutes after they entered the water Roger had the surprise of his life. Quite suddenly there was a dolphin among them. That was the first he saw of it. Diccon and Butterbeans, riding back along the shore, saw it too and shouted, waving. The three swimmers stood still in waist-high water. Tamzin held her breath; Roger wasn't absolutely sure of anyone's safety and glanced back at the shore. The dolphin glided through their group and came circling back. Only the dark, curled-back dorsal fin was out of the water. No one moved, afraid of frightening it away. Tamzin was elated and awed by a certainty that it was the same dolphin and that it had come because she was there; but as soon as the thought came to her she rejected it. The dolphin was so obviously enjoying the company of all of them. There could be no mistake about that; and an astonishing thing it was, even if it was just human company that it sought, and not a particular remembered person.

Meryon was the first to start swimming, in cautious slow circles. The dolphin began to plunge along the surface, not leaping clear but showing the long dark back and snouted head with its crescent blow-hole. The intelligent eyes, that were not fish-like, watched them all. In a minute all were swimming, and the dolphin came rollicking through and round them, under and up, with a cheerful rolling movement.

Diccon and Butterbeans had ridden girth-deep into the water and sat staring at the marvel, hardly believing their eyes. Meryon stretched out his hands as the dolphin raced past him, but it sheered away like a wild pony, and then suddenly turned and deliberately dived underneath him.

"If anyone's telling me he isn't *playing*, I shan't believe them," Roger said incredulously. He glided to meet the dolphin.

"Of course he's playing," Meryon told him. "He played like that round the *Kittiwake*."

The dolphin eluded Roger, swirling round with a slap of its tail on the surface. "And a wicked look in his eye; did you see it?" Roger exclaimed delightedly.

Tamzin stood still, watching. The dolphin's swirl

brought it close to where she stood. She put out her hands
and ran them down the length of the smooth back that
was longer than her own height. She was the only person
who had touched the dolphin, and she had touched it
three times.

Meryon was calling to her. "The second one is out
there, do you see? About thirty yards off." He was
pointing. Tamzin could hardly look, because her own
dolphin was circling round her, brushing against her as it
had brushed the boats. She took hold of the single strong
fin and found that she was holding the dolphin as one

might hold a horse; but the dolphin was staying of its own free will.

Diccon's voice went up, "Oh, please could you bring it for us to see?" He was standing in his stirrups. Butterbeans just stared through the donkey's ears: a fisherman's son, he had never expected to be confronted with such unheard-of doings in the sea.

Tamzin didn't want to shout back while the dolphin was near her; she would go and explain to them that you can't pull along by the fin someone who has saved your life, even if he should allow it. Letting the fin slip through her hands she turned to swim towards the shore.

"Look over your shoulder!" Meryon called.

She did so, and saw the dolphin swimming close behind her. It came with her nearly to Banner and Skylark; and then the donkey suddenly pawed the water with his hoof and brayed. Tamzin turned to look but the dolphin had gone. There was nothing to be seen of it. Far out, the second dolphin plunged and leaped.

Butterbeans would have hit the donkey, but Diccon shouted at him. Then Banner started rearing, thinking the shouting was at him. Tamzin waded up, trying to make peace. "You did see it quite close; you were awfully lucky, really."

"Look! Look!" Butterbeans cried, pointing seawards. "There it is!"

Her hand on Banner's bridle, Tamzin turned and saw two dolphins throwing themselves into the air, silver in the low sunlight.

"Come on, old young 'un," Meryon said, shooting up to where she stood. "I promised I'd see you didn't stay in long."

"They might come back," she said, looking at the dolphins.

"There's to-morrow evening; the next one, and the

next." He took her hand and led her firmly ashore, Skylark and Banner splashing after them.

Roger came up with a great thrashing of feet though the water here was scarcely deep enough for swimming. "One of these days she'll vanish on the dolphin's back," he said to Meryon. "I expect she's a mermaid really; a changeling, you know; and they're trying to get her back."

"Seriously," said Meryon, "the astonishing thing is that he really did seem to know Tamzin. He wouldn't let either of us touch him."

Tamzin looked back, but the water was unbroken again and there were no dolphins to be seen.

CHAPTER VII

Sussex Simo

OLD JIM had a theory that the dolphin was a female who for some reason didn't have young. "Real motherly is dolphins. I reckon she's looking fer something to mother," he said. "Knew a cat what lorst her kittens, once, and I tellee true, she brung up a litter of orphaned hedgehogs. Belonged to Shirty Smeed, she did. I lay she musta learned smartish to wash 'em the way of the spines."

Every evening that week Tamzin and Meryon went swimming off the beach banks, often with friends or family, and every evening the dolphin came to meet them. Sometimes the second dolphin was in attendance, though always keeping its distance. But Tamzin's dolphin grew bolder each day. There was now no doubt at all that Tamzin herself was the favoured one, though any swimmer was greeted with friendliness. More and more people came to see the marvel, not only swimmers but shore watchers, too.

Tamzin and Meryon read all that they could find about dolphins, hunting in school and public libraries. Tamzin began keeping a dolphin note-book in which she copied the things they found. Meryon had Advanced Level examinations immediately ahead of him, and would ordinarily have been doing a fair amount of revision in the evenings; but now that he was caught up in the affair of Tamzin's dolphin he hardly worked at all.

"It doesn't really matter," he said to her when they were walking down the sea wall after school. "Actually I think I do better if I haven't been swotting just before exams."

It was Wednesday, only two days after the first swim with the dolphin, but already the news had gone round. There were at least a dozen people on the sea wall besides themselves, walking ahead or behind them and sometimes turning to look at Tamzin. She knew perfectly well that she was being discussed, and it made her a little uneasy. "Not really because of myself," she said to Meryon, "though it is queer to find yourself an object of local interest, but because perhaps it mightn't do the dolphin any good. I don't know how to express it. I don't even know how anyone might hurt her, even if they wanted to. It's funny," she added, her sandals brushing the miniature foxgloves that grew along the mud wall, "but I never thought of the possibility of so many people coming to see her. Did you?"

"I didn't think of it, but now they're coming I do see why. Anything like this catches the imagination. The age-old problem of man communicating with the animals, I suppose. And remember Pelorus Jack; how people went from all over the world to see him escort the steamers." Meryon's towel was round his shoulders, his white school shirt was open and the sleeves rolled up.

Tamzin said, "Pelorus Jack. I've got a name for my dolphin, too, a really ancient name. Father found it. He was reading in Pliny's *Natural History* about dolphins, and Pliny says that because their snouts are turned up they all answer ' in a surprising manner ' to the name of Simo. It means Snubnose, and he says they ' like it better than any other.' Pliny must have been rather nice, think. I'm going to call my dolphin Sussex Simo, hough it sounds a bit masculine for a she-dolphin."

Meryon smiled at her. "I think Pliny would have been pleased; his name being used again after nineteen centuries."

Down on the shore more people were waiting, sitting in little groups or walking along the wet sand left by the ebbing tide. Four or five bathers were in the water playing with a beach-ball, and a young woman with a large black dog splashed about in the shallows. Tamzin looked in dismay as she and Meryon came over the beach banks. "She'll never come, with all these people. It's worse every evening."

"She likes people," Meryon said. "Though, sensible creature, she likes you best."

"We could go in a little farther up. Not nearer the river because of the undercurrent, but the other way."

"Well, of course: but the people will only follow you. You're news now, you and Sussex Simo."

Meryon was absolutely right. They were hardly in the water before people began to move along, some with cameras held ready and some with binoculars. The bathers, too, were wading nearer with their ball, and more sightseers had appeared on the beach banks from the sea wall path.

Tamzin dived into a wave and swam out quickly. "It's like being a kind of Bearded Lady, sixpence a look," she said to Meryon when they were far enough out to feel less closely observed. "Now I know what tigers feel like in zoos."

He said, grinning at her as they floated, "Most people would be rather thrilled to be the centre of so much interest. But you're very unlike most people."

"It's Simo I'm thinking of." And suddenly Simo was there. She had a very sudden way of appearing. "Simo!" Tamzin called, using the name for the first time, and full of delight and relief in the dolphin's appearance and her unmistakable friendliness.

"Her mate is out there," Meryon said, seeing the arching back and dorsal fin a little to seawards.

Tamzin was too much occupied with Simo to spare more than a glance for the lone dolphin who never came nearer. Simo was behaving like a dog who has just found a lost mistress again. She took almost no notice of Meryon, though no longer deliberately avoiding him, but she nosed Tamzin's hands as she swam round her.

"You can *see* how pleased she is!" Tamzin cried. "Would you ever have thought a dolphin could show it so clearly?"

"I should never have thought a dolphin could do any of the things she does," he said, and then noticed that the bathers were coming towards them with their ball. The tide was low enough for the water to be chest-high where they were. Meryon stood straddled for a moment, looking back at the shore-watchers with their cameras and the approaching bathers while Simo swam round Tamzin. He heard the "whoosh" of air from her blow-hole as she breathed; and then suddenly she had dived through his legs and tipped him backwards into the sea. As he came up spluttering the dolphin turned back in a graceful swirl, slapping her tail down on the water as she sailed back past him to drench him again.

Meryon pushed back his streaming hair and rubbed his eyes. Simo was close to Tamzin again. Tamzin's hand was on the shining dark back as she stood laughing. Meryon turned a careless somersault in the water. "Just to show her she needn't think she's the only one who's at home under water!" He paused a moment. "But, Tamzin, do you realise that this is momentous? It's almost certain proof that dolphins have a sense of humour.

That was as much horseplay as Rissa ducking Roger, or a dog running off with a slipper."

Tamzin was floating beside the dolphin, holding Simo's dorsal fin and being gently towed. They both knew that this, too, was another marvellous thing; but they were getting used to, and almost expecting, marvellous things. She said, "If dogs can play, with their small brains, of course dolphins can. Father says their brains are bigger than ours. And we saw them playing round the boats."

The bathers had come up near enough to call to Tamzin, now.

"Is it a porpoise? I never heard of a tame one! Is it yours?" This was a young woman in a yellow cap and ruched orange swim-suit. A very brown-skinned muscular man with her added, "Everyone in Dunsford's talking about it. Did you know there's a reporter from the local rag up there, waiting to see you?"

"It does look sweet! Can we stroke it?" a plump girl with the beach-ball asked.

Meryon thought that Simo would shy away from the bathers, but the dolphin seemed almost to ignore them, rolling gently around Tamzin with lazy flips of her powerful tail-flukes. Tamzin said a little anxiously, "She's an ordinary wild dolphin. I don't really know why she's so friendly with me; but I think she might go away if too many people come close to her."

The girl with the ball said, "Oh, we won't come too close." Then suddenly she tossed her ball to the dolphin. Before anyone could say or do anything Simo was nosing at the ball. "There!" said the girl, "she likes it! Isn't she cute? Come on, here, here!" she called, as if Simo were a dog retrieving a stick.

The dolphin took no notice of this, but went on pushing the ball about, coming close to Meryon as she did so. He put a hand under the ball and flipped it up out of the water a little. Simo rushed forward to meet it and then flipped it up herself, with a toss of her head. Cries of admiration went up from the bathers. The girl in the yellow cap splashed with her hands, calling the dolphin. Five more bathers were running into the water from the beach, which was now more crowded with onlookers than Tamzin remembered ever seeing it, even on a fine August Bank Holiday. Several of the village people were there, too. Tamzin recognised among others members of the large Lillycrop family, and even surprisingly Hookey Galley, a very taciturn fisherman. She was faintly uneasy about this, as trouble often followed where Hookey went. There were two of the coastguards, and old Jim's young Jimmy, and Charlie Deeprose who owned the village's only farm.

Simo went on tossing the ball, amusing herself; she seemed to be unaware of all the interest she was causing. Tamzin caught the ball once or twice and tossed it back. Simo was playing only with her. When anyone else threw the ball she merely took it away, pushing it with her snout as a footballer dribbles with his boot; but when Tamzin threw it she tossed it back. Meryon noticed at once the accuracy of the dolphin's throw; she was far more precise than any of the people playing with her. Sometimes she reared herself half out of the water to see exactly where the ball was.

When the other bathers arrived the play began to get rather rough. People were splashing the dolphin, and throwing the ball at her rather than to her. Tamzin and Meryon tried to explain that this might drive her away, but the brown muscular man said, "Go on! She's enjoying it," and he grabbed at her tail. Simo whipped the tail from his hands and slapped it down hard on the water; and then she was gone, slipping under silently and smoothly.

The bathers gazed around blankly. Tamzin and Meryon looked away farther, and in a moment saw two dark curved fins break the water. Tamzin thought she heard the quick explosive "Ph-HOOP" of a dolphin breathing.

"I didn't think she'd stand for much of that," Meryon said.

Now that Simo was gone Tamzin only wanted to go, herself. She looked at the crowds, who were all looking at her, and suddenly felt that she wanted to escape, as Simo had escaped. Meryon understood the look and said, "But you can't just slide out to sea; you've got to go back through them all. Never mind, they'll have to capture me before they can really molest you."

All the same the journey home, even with Meryon, was bothersome enough for Tamzin to wonder what it might have been like without him. They were accosted by the local reporter before they were properly out of the water. "I'm from the *Sussex Tribune*, I wonder if you could spare me a few minutes?"

People pushed round them, goggling, listening, asking questions of their own. It was hopeless thinking of dressing as they usually did, under towels. Wrapping the towels round them they picked up their clothes and walked on, answering questions as they went. Tamzin's damp hair hung round her shoulders, darkened to corn-colour by the sea.

"Is it true that the dolphin saved your life, Miss Grey?"

"Could you just stand still for one moment, for a photograph?"

"What does the dolphin do when you're at school? And what about the winter?"

"What do your parents think? And what do you think the dolphin thinks? What was the name you called her?"

Meryon answered most of them, in his own particular evasive way: he could be very evasive when he wanted.

Tamzin was grateful. She might almost have felt happy: these last few days had been incredible and wonderful days for her; only one thing worried her. When at last they had shut the vicarage gates and were walking alone past the tamarisks and Mr. Grey's roses, she said, "I can't help thinking that there might be some danger to Simo in all this. If only we hadn't said anything to anyone in the beginning!"

"You needn't think," he said, "that a marvel like this could have been kept quiet for long. Sooner or later someone would have known; and then everyone would have known, just the same as now."

At the door she said anxiously, "What about when it gets into the papers?"

He squeezed her hand reassuringly. "Probably the weather will break."

CHAPTER VIII

To See the Dolphin

READING in bed that night in her father's translation of Pliny, Tamzin found with joy the story of an earlier Simo and a schoolboy whose name Pliny seemed to have forgotten. This boy, who lived near Naples, used to walk round a long sea-inlet to his school on the other side. A dolphin came to the inlet and developed a great affection for the boy. It would come to him, said Pliny, even if it were at the bottom of the water when he called to it with the Romans' pet-name for all dolphins, "Simo! Simo!"

One day when the boy was swimming he got on to the dolphin's back, and the dolphin carried him proudly. For years afterwards it used to wait for him and carry him across the sea-creek to school, and back again in the evening; until a time when suddenly the boy did not appear. The dolphin came looking for him every morning, as it had always done, but the boy had fallen ill and died. Realising this at last the dolphin also died, of sorrow and regret for its lost friend.

Tamzin was grief-stricken at the sad ending of the story, just as if it had not all happened nearly 2,000 years ago. She felt too old to cry but the tears still came, as they always did when she read sad books, like *Tess of the D'Urbervilles*, and she buried her face in her pillow. Thinking of her own Simo she wondered what might happen if one day she didn't go down to the beach banks.

I'll always go, she told herself, as long as Simo's there. I'll swim or row or sail, whatever the weather. She was ashamed to remember a moment when she had almost decided to stay away because of the crowds of gazing, curious people. Turning out her light she fell asleep making up a poem about a dolphin.

At breakfast in the kitchen the next morning Tamzin was still preoccupied with her poem, which was proving difficult: dolphin was not an easy word to rhyme. She wasn't taking much notice of Diccon who was trying to draw her into an argument about holes, while bolting his scrambled egg.

"What I want to know is, when is a hole not a hole? Well, I mean, this is a hole, isn't it?" jabbing a finger at the top of the salt-pot, "but is this a hole?" looking into the marmalade jar, "or even that?" pointing to the coffee-pot spout. "Take caves—Tamzin, you aren't listening!"

"If you don't hurry up with your egg we'll be late for school."

Then the telephone rang. Tamzin's father went to answer it but came back at once. "It's for you. It's the *Daily News.*"

"For *me*?"

"They want to know about your dolphin."

"Oh, *no*!" Tamzin cried. "If it gets into the London papers more and more people will come down, and drive her away. Please tell them I'd rather not!"

The vicar considered this for a second and then said, "I don't think it would do any good. They're bound to print something, in any case, and it might be better if it's something you've said, rather than something they feel they must invent."

Mrs. Grey glanced anxiously at the clock on the mantel-piece. "Ten minutes before you have to start for school."

"We're riding and the ponies are ready," Tamzin said as she got up and went to the telephone.

Johnny Beatup, handsome son of Westling's fattest woman, came with the papers while she was just saying, "This is Tamzin Grey." Throwing them in at the open front door he rushed off; he too was driven by the inflexible hour of school. Diccon came running down the hall to pounce on the papers while Johnny's feet still pounded up the drive.

"Yes, she does," Tamzin was saying on the telephone, "but please don't print any more than you can help because of people coming down."

"It's in!" shouted Diccon, fluttering pages as he walked down the hall. "Two photographs of Tamzin, one with the dolphin, and a whole lot about it all."

Tamzin groaned, and then said into the phone, "No, it was only me groaning, about another paper."

At school she found herself suddenly the centre of interest. This was a strange enough experience, since she and Rissa were used to thinking of themselves as odd ones out; people who preferred messing about barefooted in boats to watching television, who kept their finger-nails short and wore old flat sandals and couldn't be bothered with teenage crazes. Tamzin, of course, had always been rather envied for riding to school. The pupils seldom saw Cascade, who was stabled in the town with Banner; but Tamzin's old jodhpurs, which she was allowed to change at school, were enough to start people thinking of galloping hoofs and flying manes. At Diccon's school the reverse was the case. The main interest that year was sports cars. Diccon was thought a little old-fashioned to come to school so often on a pony when everyone else came in buses or cars.

Not waiting for tea Meryon changed quickly into swim-trunks and week-end clothes as soon as he got home, and went out to get his bicycle. The house where he lived was an old one, built in the Sussex tradition with pinky-orange tiles on the roof and half-way down the walls. It was covered with Virginia creeper, green now but flaming crimson in the autumn; it was hidden in trees and beset with shrubs and flowers.

Apart from Meryon's parents the house had one other inhabitant, Meryon's half-grown brown Burmese kitten which he called Burma since he didn't know any Burmese names. As well as having a craze for and playing with—and even sitting in—water, this kitten spent much time adding to what was known in the family as his collection. He was doing this as Meryon passed him on the way to the bicycle shed. This time it was an enormous magnolia leaf which had caught his fancy, but it was so big and up-curled that it obstructed his view and he was shuffling backwards with it. "I shouldn't think that can improve visibility much," Meryon remarked to him as they passed, but Burma continued regardless. He always carried large things backwards.

Meryon rode down the drive to meet Roger in a blaze of heat-wave sunshine. Well, so much for a break in the weather, he said to himself; what with this and the local rag there'll be some people on the beach this evening, I'm thinking; but with any luck they won't see us.

There was a new plan for the evening, worked out by Tamzin and Meryon and Tamzin's parents at supper the evening before. It was that they should go down to swim much farther along the lonely shore, beyond the lifeboat house. No crowds would be there, and probably at first no dolphin; but the vicar believed it was possible that the dolphin might swim to Tamzin if she were anywhere at all in the bay.

"In any case," he said, "it could be an extremely interesting experiment. If Simo doesn't appear, you have only missed a day; if she does, you may be able to hold off the crowds for a day or two, as well as having evidence of the remarkable range-finding powers that are being claimed for dolphins."

Tamzin had been uneasy about the plan; she didn't want to look on Simo as an experiment. "All I can think is that she saved me; and because she seems to like to see me I can thank her, in a kind of way, by going. And of course I want to see her, too; anybody would; she's so gentle and quick and, oh, so intelligent, like the best horses."

But in the end Tamzin agreed to try the idea. She and Diccon on their ponies and Rissa on her bicycle rode straight from school to Castle Farm by the cart-track over the Marsh. At the farm, which was a half-way point to the beach, Rissa changed over to her own pony and all three rode on to the sea.

The Running Wind had dried the rich grass of the Marsh until it was browned and tawny like a lion's back. Mysterious islands of shingle appeared in the grazings here and there, only a little more golden than the grass. The sky seemed full of larks. It was sightseers' weather all right, and sure enough on the distant sea wall path a long trail of people could be seen winding down to the shore. Out to the west two bicycles crawled along a sheep-track, one behind the other, the sun glinting on wheels and handlebars. Between bicycles and trailing snake of sight-seers the three ponies cantered, heading for the sea.

There was no one, no one at all on the lonely stretch of beach by the lifeboat house. It was high water, with the tide right up the shingle. The boys' bicycles were already propped against the lifeboat house when the ponies came up. Roger appeared round the corner of the building as they were tying the ponies to the winch that was used to haul in the lifeboat. "I suppose you've seen the fly-paper? Beach is black with people down that end."

"Well, we saw the procession." Rissa gave Siani's halter-rope a tightening tug and went round to look from the other side.

Meryon was standing there. He glanced over his shoulder. "How many do you think? Three hundred? Or more? And all to see the dolphin."

Tamzin had joined them: Diccon was already pulling off his clothes behind the lifeboat house; hot and dusty he was longing for the water. She gazed in silence at the multitude, thinking how Biblical it seemed in some strange way; but it was not a prophet that they had trudged the miles to see. Her eyes went out to the water shimmering under the sun; it too was crowded with people. Because she was looking beyond them for a sign of Simo she was not the first to see a donkey-cart move out and in again among the crowd.

"Well, would you believe that?" Rissa said. "It can only be Jim. And I wouldn't mind betting that he's selling ice-cream to the mob."

Tamzin's glance shot back to the beach disbelievingly. "He wouldn't, when he knows how worried we are——" Then she too saw the donkey and cart. Certainly Jim was selling something, most probably not fish.

"There you are," said Rissa, "making a profit out of your misfortune, the old hoodwinker. I suppose young Jimmy's been left to look after the ferry."

"He's got to make a profit out of something!" Tamzin sprang automatically to his defence, as she always had, but she ached inside. And because she was looking at the donkey-cart she was not the first to see Simo.

"Your dolphin," said Meryon, "is playing with the bathers. Look!"

Diccon came running up in his swim-trunks. "I saw

the dolphin! She jumped right out of the water. Look, there she is again! So much for breaking her heart like the Pliny one you read about, Tamzin; she plays with anyone," he said with the unconscious cruelty of the young.

Suddenly Tamzin felt doubly betrayed, by Jim and by her dolphin. "Anyway, let's go swimming," she said, whirling round. "I bet I'll be changed before any of you!"

· At this part of the beach the breakwaters stood high, hiding the five of them from the distant crowd as they ran into the sea. They might have imagined themselves the only people on the whole long coast, except for the faraway noise of shouting and laughter from the dolphin's admirers. Roger had brought a ball for Simo to play with, but she was playing with those others a mile away down the beach.

"The tide's high enough for a mock-up water-polo,"
he said, trying to cheer up Tamzin. "Really we ought to
have anchored inner-tubes, or something, for goals, but
we could use two uprights in the breakwater. Meryon
and I against you three."

Tamzin played with tremendous gusto, diving with
the ball, attacking the enemy and scoring the first and
only goal. She didn't want to think about Simo and old
Jim defecting to the adulating sightseers. She didn't
want to remember any of those dolphins of history who
had stayed faithful only to one person. There was, too,
she remembered in spite of herself, another New Zealand
dolphin, called Opo, who had died only a few years ago;
the second dolphin in the world to be protected by an
Order in Council;

Like the others this dolphin had attached herself to one
person, Jill Baker, who was then about her own age.

When Jill was in the water, so Tamzin and Meryon had been reading, Opo would have nothing to do with any other swimmer, though hundreds might be there. Remembering and trying not to remember, Tamzin jumped with fright at a sudden explosion as Simo leaped out of the water right in front of her.

"Pff-HOO-p," came from the dolphin's blow-hole as she expelled and took in air.

"Simo!" Tamzin cried.

Meryon pushed his wet hair back with both hands, treading water and watching. "As I once remarked before, she plays with anyone but, sensible creature, prefers you."

The dolphin whirled round Tamzin. Diccon threw the ball to her and she sent it high in the air, racing forward to be under it when it came down. No one knew where the lone dolphin was.

"Probably still waiting around at the sea wall end, poor thing," Rissa said.

"Oh, could I try riding Simo, like Pliny's boy?" Diccon pleaded.

"I suppose you could," agreed Tamzin. Simo was so gay this evening she might consent to almost anything. In shallower water Tamzin lifted him up and set him in front of the big dorsal fin. "Hold on to her flippers; but gently. And don't shout."

"I'm riding! I'm really riding a real dolphin!" he suddenly said in a hoarse loud whisper. "Just like the boy in the book." And so he was.

Far down the shore the crowd still stood waiting, wondering where their dolphin had gone.

The lone dolphin was in attendance again before Simo finally took her leave, the two of them rollicking through the waves into the distance.

"I wonder what her mate thinks of it all?" Roger said

when they were dry and changed and sprawling on the hot shingle under a descending sun. "Perhaps he feels like a man who's married a fairy, afraid to follow when she goes to play with strange creatures."

Meryon lay spread-eagled looking up at a pattern of mackerel clouds and seagulls. "A thing that puzzles me is how quickly Simo began playing with us. Other dolphins have played with bathers; but they all seem to have taken some time in getting used to people, first."

Rissa said, "I suppose she could be one of those other dolphins. Not one of the ones we've read about, of course, but just a dolphin who played with bathers somewhere else; last winter, say, when dolphins would all have gone off to warmer water, such as the Mediterranean."

Tamzin was still gazing at the sea. It was the kind of logical thing Rissa would suggest, she thought, not really wanting to consider it because it weakened the strange and wonderful link between her and Simo; but she knew that it was probably true. She knew, too, that if it was so it was really a thing to be glad about, rather than sorry. Wasn't it better that her dolphin should feel friendliness towards all people instead of only to herself? All the same, it needed a better and wiser human than she was, not to feel a pang of wistfulness at the thought.

Turning to look at her Meryon knew how she felt. It was the feeling of the man who, thinking his is a one-man dog, sees it galloping off with someone else. Impossible not to feel a small hurt. He remembered something he had read and noted down for Tamzin the night before.

"I found a thing in Plutarch," he said, rolling over to delve in his pocket. "Here it is; I copied it out for your dolphin note-book."

In Meryon's black ink and angular handwriting she read:

"To the dolphin alone, beyond all others, nature has granted what the best philosophers seek, friendship for no advantage. Though it has no need at all of any man, yet it is a genial friend to all and has helped many."

"But of course," said Meryon, understanding, "even a dolphin can have a best friend."

CHAPTER IX

The Great Invasion

TAMZIN and Diccon rode home late that evening, after the day-long absence at school and on the beach, and they did the ponies before going in to their own supper. Tamzin was happy, in a tired dreamy way that not even the ferryman's defection could dull. Both she and Diccon were drowsy with long activity and drugged with sun and sea-water. Their faces were browner and Tamzin's dusty freckles darker than the day before.

"It's Saturday to-morrow," she said with a yawn pulling off Cascade's saddle; "let's clean the tack in the morning."

Over supper she was telling her parents how Simo had found them near the lifeboat house; she had half-forgotten about the reporters.

"And I *rode* on her, I really did!" Diccon said. "She was slippery as eels but I held on by her flippers."

There was so much to tell, neither of them had thought that there might be news at the vicarage end, too.

"I'm afraid your great crowd is bound to get bigger," the vicar said. "Five reporters have been here, to-day; and although we told them as little as we could, Simo almost certainly will be in all the London papers in the morning; there's no help for it."

The cheerfulness went from Tamzin's face. "Oh, Dad." But Diccon thought the news exciting.

"Four of the reporters went on down to the beach,"

Mrs. Grey told them. "I expect they saw Simo before she found you, so there may be photographs, too. They asked if you would be there."

"What did you say?"

"That you'd gone riding after school and were not back yet."

"Smiling Morn and old Jim have been doing quite nicely out of it," the vicar observed. "The whole of the main street has been lined with parked cars for most of the evening. Smiling Morn kept the shop open to sell ice-cream and sweets and so forth to the people. No soft drinks because Jim foresaw the possibilities and bought him out earlier. He took a donkey-cart load down to the beach, where I dare say he sold it at exorbitant prices."

"Oh, so that was what he was selling."

"Bed for you, young man; it's hours past your time," Mrs. Grey said to Diccon, and bore him off as soon as he had finished his last spoonful of raspberries and junket.

Tamzin copied Meryon's quotation from Plutarch into her dolphin note-book, and then sat drawing horses on scrap paper for a while to take her mind off anxieties about all the publicity for Simo. Horses were the thing she liked drawing best, so she drew them better than anything else; but she never could learn to draw hoofs, and always made all her horses stand fetlock deep in long grass to avoid the difficulty altogether. When presently, she found herself drawing dolphins she pushed the pencil away and read until bedtime.

As the vicar had predicted, all the London newspapers had accounts of Sussex Simo in the morning. Johnny Beatup showed them to Tamzin at the front door when he brought the vicarage paper. Suddenly she saw Simo and herself in headlines. "Dolphin Girl Evades Crowds." "Sussex Simo Plays for People." "Hundreds on Sussex Dolphin Beach." "Elusive Tamzin Grey, the Dolphin

Girl." There were photographs, too, of Simo playing with the bathers, and of the crowds that jostled on the beach. She looked at them in awe and despair, though already planning to cut them out for her note-book.

"That's me, there," said Johnny proudly, stubbing his finger on to the paper, "and that's Mr. Decks with his donkey-cart, see, selling pop; and the Lillycrops was just out of the picture, that's Min's elbow. I bet we get a bigger crowd'n ever, now, don't you?"

Tamzin said yes, she supposed they might, and then Meryon rang up to ask if she had seen the papers. "Another thing I thought of," he said, "is that you're awfully likely to be seen by someone, riding out to our part of the beach. There's going to be a great pilgrimage, if I'm not very much mistaken; it's a Saturday, and the news in pretty well all the papers."

"Yes, but what?"

"How about coming to lunch? Mother and Dad are always glad to see you. Then we could pick up Roger and go in the *Emma:* Rissa says she's riding. We'd never be noticed going from here and parking *Emma* at the road end. I've saved enough for a spot of petrol; it's a pity she uses such a lot."

"All right! I'll come on Cascade. Really I ought to clean his tack, after yesterday."

"Leave it till this evening and I'll help you."

Already cars had begun flowing into the village. Old Jim had been out early roping off a part of the hard near his ferry hut which he marked, with chalk on a board, 'Parking a Bob." Three cars were in it by half past ten, when Tamzin rode away on Cascade. From that time the great invasion began. Westling had never seen anything like it. Cars and bicycles and buses came down the long road from Dunsford. Motor bicycles and vans and hot lusty people on foot came streaming in as the invasion mounted. There were soon no more spaces at the road-side, and villagers who had pieces of ground were letting them out for parking. Anyone who cared to make money could do so; there were people looking for rooms for the week-end, people looking for camping sites, for a meal, for a drink, for repairs to cars and bicycles, for all the things that people could possibly want on a hot July Saturday when they were far away from home.

Tamzin saw little of this, but her family scarcely stopped answering the door all the morning. Everyone wanted to see Tamzin; not only the reporters. Would she appear an television? Would she write her own account of the events for a daily paper? Please, would she sign her autograph?—dozens of autographs? Could she be seen by appointment, and if so, when? Had Mrs. Grey a recent photograph she would lend for reproduction? Could she say where her daughter was now? And could she give some details about Tamzin's life and character, please?

Meanwhile, untroubled, Tamzin rode on across the tawny-dry grazings, working out her dolphin poem and wondering if it would turn out good enough to go into her note-book.

> *Dolphin leaping in a moonlit wave,*
> *Swift and gentle you came to save.*
> *Dolphin racing on a summer's day,*
> *Remembering, you came to play. . . .*

At Meryon's house she practised hand-stands on the lawn with him, helped his mother to make a salad and inspected and admired the Burmese kitten's collection. She would have been astonished to hear that so many people were at that minute clamouring to know where she was.

"I've started my own note-book, now," Meryon said

as they drove away in the *Emma* after lunch. "It's my Tamzin Grey newspaper cutting book! And, I say, could I by any chance have your autograph? It's an awful long time since you wrote me a letter."

"Gump!" said Tamzin, using Rissa's favourite disparagement.

Surprisingly, Rissa was not the only person on their strip of beach when they got there. A family of four was established under the breakwater; father and mother and two small girls aged about four and six. From their peaceful absorption in their own affairs of sand-pies and tide-pools and sun-bathing it seemed as if they had not even heard about the dolphin. The tide was far out over the sands, though coming in quickly now. Already the distant shore was dark with people, and the sea wall carried its long slow snake.

Rissa said, "Hallo, Dolphin Girl! If they ever put me in the papers I'll sue them. Doesn't it make you sick?"

"No, it only frightens me a bit in case of danger to Simo. I can't really honestly think that anyone would want to hurt her, but I still feel uneasy." She was gazing at the far crowd, stretching down the hard sand now to the tide's edge and into the shallow water. The donkey-cart was there, and more people than Tamzin could remember ever seeing in one place at one time before; but there was no visible sign of Simo. The family party by the breakwater must have been aware of the multitude, but they took no notice. Perhaps they were strangers to this coast and thought that it was always like that, and were glad to have found a quiet corner.

"They're staying at the Watch Houses," Rissa said, when she and Tamzin were changing. "I rode down to bathe Siani's legs in the sea and they came across to give her some sugar, and we talked for a bit."

When Rissa and Tamzin and the boys ran down over the

wet sand that was cool and wind-ridged under their feet, the little girls were being helped into frilly cotton swim-suits.

"It looks as if Simo will soon have company," Roger said, "whichever end of the shore she comes."

"If she comes," said Rissa. "There doesn't seem to be any sign of her at all in the bay, to-day."

"She won't mind the little girls; it's the big rough hoodlums who grab at her she hates," Tamzin said, her feet splashing into the small running waves. She wasn't concerned with the idea that Simo might not come. The other three all had their doubts, but Tamzin ran ahead into the sea, calling, "Simo!"

CHAPTER X

The Running Mob

So QUICKLY did Simo shoot up from the water, she could not have been far away when Tamzin called.

"She was waiting for you, just off-shore, that's what. Probably never been along to her other admirers all day." Roger threw himself down in the shining water, swimming beside Tamzin and the dolphin. Tamzin was holding Simo's flipper, being towed through the water. Meryon came thrashing up and dived under them, with Rissa close behind. They were all used to playing with Simo now. She enjoyed this and was not above quite rough horseplay of the ducking and splashing variety in return; but with Tamzin she was always gentle.

Tamzin said, "If Jim's right about her being a female who's lost her young or didn't have one this year, perhaps it's just because I'm the smallest." But really she was certain that it was because Simo had saved her life.

It now became obvious that the solitary parents had somehow not heard about the dolphin. In their swim-suits they came running down to the water holding the children's hands, and they all looked as astonished as if they had seen a mermaid rise from the sea. In the shallow water they picked up their daughters and came closer, staring incredulously. He was tall and blond and she was tall and dark, and both the little girls had brown hair— one curly and one straight—brown eyes and sun-browned skins. The same old questions were shot at Tamzin and the others.

"It it a tame one? What kind of fish is it? Do you think we could come closer?"

Roger looked at them disbelievingly. "It's a dolphin. She's been in all the papers, haven't you seen?"

"We haven't seen any papers all the week; it makes it more of a holiday," the fair man explained. "The Watch Houses are pretty lonely, and there's nobody in the other one until August; we're the only family staying there." He was holding the smaller child, the curly one.

"That's what all that crowd is there for," Rissa told them, glancing down the shore. "It's been going on for days. And that's why we're up at this end; to play with the dolphin in peace. She's called Simo," she added.

The two children were enchanted. They stretched out their hands and begged to be put down in the water.

"Do you think it would be safe?" their mother asked. "Susan can swim a little, but not Mary, yet. They would love to pat the dolphin, if she'd let them."

"I should think it'd be all right," said Meryon. "She seems very gentle."

Tamzin said, "Dolphins are the gentlest animals there are." Her arm was over Simo's back.

"We-ell," said the children's mother, and in a second Susan was splashing through the water, followed cautiously at first by Mary still holding her father's hand.

Simo was plainly delighted. She kept herself still while the children patted and stroked her, but her expressive eyes followed them with obvious pleasure. Tamzin lifted Susan on to Simo's back and Simo swam in slow circles, as pleased and as gentle as could be, with Tamzin wading at her side holding Susan. Meryon had been slightly uneasy in case Simo began any of her rough splashing games, but it seemed that the smaller her companions the gentler she became.

"She has such an attractive face," the children's mother

said, "the way her mouth curves up in a kind of smiling expression. It gives her a benign look."

With little Mary, held on her back by her father, Simo hardly moved at all.

"Oh, why do we don't have one of these at home?" Mary pleaded.

"I must go and get the camera!" her mother exclaimed. The small curly child on the dolphin was a sight to be preserved for all their lives.

"What luck," said the father, "to think of coming on her by accident, when hundreds of people are looking for her."

Tamzin glanced back along the shore when he mentioned the people. She froze where she stood beside Simo at the shock of what she saw. The whole great crowd,

like a wave of lava, was sweeping down the beach towards them. The others looked, too. Everyone had been too absorbed in the dolphin to think about the people before.

"It's because the tide's low," Meryon said. "Anyone with binoculars could easily see that we had Simo here."

Tamzin swung round. "But what can we do?"

"Nothing. We've always known they'd get on to it sooner or later. I can't see that it really matters, except that it's nice to have Simo to ourselves. She likes the gentle admirers, and she's pretty well able to deal, herself, with the roughs. We'd better just make up our minds to share her."

"Honestly," said Rissa, "I can't see what harm you think they can do to her."

"Surely nobody would want to," the children's father said, "she's such a delightful creature."

Mary and Susan were now jumping around Simo with affectionate gusto. She received their lively advances with the utmost gentleness, as if realising their youth and irresponsibility. She was like a big gentle sheepdog being played with by boisterous puppies. Tamzin was looking across her to the horde of her admirers who advanced dark and fast like locusts over the beach. Already nearly gone were the quiet idyllic hours. Never again would they be able to hide Simo from her doting public. In a few minutes now she would be everyone's dolphin, for as long as she stayed in the bay.

Afraid that Simo might become nervous or excited by the swiftly approaching crowd, Mary's mother lifted her off the dolphin's back.

"Oh, but Mary didn't went as far as Susan!" the small girl wailed.

"I'll give you a ride on my back, if you like," Meryon offered, "and you can pretend that I'm a sea-horse."

Roger came up from an underwater glide to see the

progress of the rushing advance. "They may not have any four-minute milers there, but I bet there are several sixers. The spear-head will be with us any moment, now."

"I'm going to make sure Siani's all right," Rissa said, remembering what had happened once before.

"Mind you don't get trampled by the thundering herd," Roger called after her as she ran splashing through shallow waves.

"I wonder if we ought to get the children to the shore, dear," said their father. "And there are all our things up by the breakwater."

"It's all right, duckies, you can come and play with Simo again," their mother consoled them, sweeping the small one up into her arms.

Tamzin watched them wade out to the sand, far behind Rissa's running figure. She was aware of the old strong urge to escape, herself, somewhere away from all these people that were like an army advancing to attack; but she couldn't leave Simo. Her glance moved from the frightening scene on the shore to the quiet horizon, a hazy distant line under the hot sun.

Meryon said, "Don't go riding Simo out to sea."

Tamzin always wondered at the way he knew what she was thinking. "Wouldn't it be nice if we could? Her mate is out there—a dolphin each."

"They're on us, chaps," Roger said, staring at the shore. "At least, the forefront of the battle. Rearguard coming up fast; kids, dogs, mums, spades, even Jim and the fish-cart. I expect he can't stop Skylark."

Simo was amusing herself playing with the water-polo ball. She had been pushing it deep under the water with her snout and then leaving go so that it shot up quite high in the air, then she rushed to be under it as it fell. Now, presumably hearing the shouts and cries from the shore, she reared herself out of the water, as she could do so easily, and saw the situation for herself.

"There she is! There she is!" the cry went up from the beach. People in swim-suits were dashing into the sea again after the long run down the shore. The younger and stronger seemed little affected by the strenuous exercise under the blazing sun, but others flopped exhausted on the beach and many were still plodding behind; the fat and the elderly, the loaded and the unwisely shod.

Tamzin glanced uneasily at Simo, to see what she would do; but Simo loved an audience, she liked crowds and laughter. Suddenly she leapt out of the water in a curving graceful arc, and then again and again, higher and higher. Sunlit water fell from her, and the sun gleamed along her dark sides. The people howled their pleasure, pointing and crowding close along the tide-line. The bathers were close round Simo now, tossing her ball to her, tossing their own balls; some reached out to touch her as she swirled past.

Tamzin and Meryon swam out a little, pretending not to hear shouts for "The Dolphin Girl"; but Roger stayed among the bathers, finding it entertaining to listen to their exclamations. Simo darted between Tamzin and the crowd, rollicking in the water with a kind of gay abandon. Then the astonishing thing happened. Rissa could scarcely believe it as she came running from behind the lifeboat house. Behind the bathers people with bare feet and rolled-up trousers had waded out knee-deep: now suddenly they surged forward, first one and then a dozen or more. In all their clothes they pressed through the deepening water with hands stretched out to touch the dolphin.

To Rissa running down through gaping crowds to the sea it was as if people had taken leave of their senses. But to Tamzin the scene had almost a religious quality, as of a crowd pushing into the sea to touch a prophet's garment. Once before she had thought of Simo and the crowd on the shore in this way, and said so now to Meryon.

"There might even be something in that," he said, "if a prophet is one who brings a message to the people. The thing everyone notices most about Simo is her gentleness and friendliness. Perhaps that is her message."

Whether this was so or not, the crowd did seem in some way to be catching her peaceful friendliness. People who had thrust past each other into the sea now played with the dolphin gently. The mob that had rushed shouting down the shore now stood together and marvelled.

Simo herself took all this with a kind of unselfconscious graciousness. She liked people, and now did all her tricks for them, playing with balls and a blown-up inner-tube. When something she did produced a shout of applause she would leap high out of the water with an exultant flip of her tail. But she never did this near any of the bathers, and she was always especially gentle when children were close to her. Several times she let Tamzin put small ones on to her back, including Mary and Susan who were now back in the water since the crowd had calmed down enough for their parents to consider it safe.

"You know, you really are enjoying it," Meryon said with a grin.

"I suppose I am!" She was surprised at herself, after all her horror at the thought of being caught up in it. She didn't even really mind the pestering questions, now, though she would never say as much as people wanted. Some of them found it more profitable to talk to Roger and Rissa, who didn't mind scraping up and sometimes slightly embroidering odd facts about Tamzin's way with animals; how she had started them all off rescuing oiled sea-birds; defending the hoopoes which had nested at the castle; and fighting (quite literally) for doomed horses on the way to continental slaughterhouses.

People on shore did even better, in some ways, out of Diccon and Butterbeans and old Jim Decks, who told of things that would have amazed and horrified Tamzin, had she known.

"And she likes her bacon flabby," Diccon confided to an eager reporter. "Funny, isn't it, not liking it crisp? She's awfully untidy in her room, too; the stable's better, Mother says."

Butterbeans Pope recalled a time when Tamzin had had measles, and had climbed down the drainpipe from her attic window and gone off galloping on the Marsh, being tired of bed; he had himself witnessed this epic. Old Jim remembered for a crowd of customers round his cart how she had sailed with him at night in the old *Thunderer* against French poachers fishing in the bay; and how her father, the vicar himself, had been taken prisoner by the French, to be rescued by a swoop of fishermen the next day.

When Simo finally swam away, back to the lonely dolphin who waited far out, Tamzin and Rissa and the boys came ashore. Now they were all more than ever aware of the influence of their gentle dolphin over the assembly of her followers. Here was this medley of people, of all kinds and all ages, mostly unknown to each other before the arrival of the dolphin; yet all talking together about the marvel, stranger to total stranger. Those who had touched her found a ready audience, though they might have nothing more to describe than the way her skin had felt. Those through whose legs she had dived, or whose children had sat on her back, were the celebrities of the day.

It was now after four o'clock and the sun at its hottest.

The shingle quivered under heat-haze; the calm sea dazzled like melted steel. Nothing was to be seen on its surface but two or three seagulls, a fisherman's sail, and a steamer that seemed to float along the sky, so veiled in heat was the horizon. The people settled down on the warm pebbles to the tea they had brought or the drinks and chocolate that old Jim sold them from his cart. Now that he saw Tamzin seemed to be enjoying herself among them the old man felt his conscience nagging him less and began to hope that she might forgive him fairly promptly, or even overlook his defection altogether.

The multitude still had only one thought: would the dolphin come back? Sitting in rows and groups on the beach banks while the tide swallowed up the hard sand, they watched the sea as they talked about Simo; but no swift curved fin broke the water. Presently Rissa slipped away to Siani, pulling her shirt and jeans on over a swim-suit already almost dry. The others turned back towards the *Emma*. No one followed them. They had become accessible, now that they were sharing the dolphin. People were sure that they would see them all, and Simo, on the next day.

CHAPTER XI

A Gleam of Danger

ALL THROUGH the next week and into another week-end
Simo's fame and popularity grew. Every morning there
was more in the papers about her, and every evening more
people set out on the pilgrimage to Westling and the long
trudge over the saltings to the sea. Films about the
dolphin had been shown on television, and there was one
exciting evening when Tamzin herself had been inter
viewed before the television cameras. Practically every
one in Westling somehow managed to see this pro
gramme, either on their own or someone else's set. Mrs
Gudgeon at the William the Conqueror hired a set for the
evening and put it in the bar. She had the fullest house
for years; even confirmed teetotallers suddenly gave in to
the temptation of going along for a glass of lemonade

There was no television at the vicarage, but this did
not matter since Tamzin's family, as well as Meryon and
Rissa and Roger, all went with her to London. After
wards, by way of celebration, Mr. Grey took them all to
the open-air theatre at Regent's Park where they saw
A Midsummer Night's Dream. Diccon fell asleep with
exhaustion in the train coming home, and Tamzin was
travel-sick or possibly partly excitement-sick, but they
both said it was worth it.

Westling was a village used to hard times, always at the
mercy of the weather, the price of fish, or even the
occasional strange non-existence of any fish in their

waters. Mrs. Gudgeon's trade depended on the fishermen's prosperity, as did Smiling Morn's; and old Jim's
ferry depended on the weather because that was what
brought or kept at home the trippers. Now, suddenly,
it was a village of prosperity. Never had so much money
flowed into its shops and houses. If for that reason alone
the village would have idolised Simo; but in fact, all
those who were able to leave their sudden prosperous
busy-ness and go to see her for themselves soon fell for
her own irresistible character. Simo became a local
figure, a tourist attraction. Her fame began to spread
overseas, as Pelorus Jack's had done, and in other countries
people were changing their minds about their holidays
in favour of visiting England and the friendly dolphin.

Tamzin had so many letters that, even with Meryon's
help, all her spare time was not enough to answer them.
Meryon himself was in the middle of Advanced Level
examinations; but he said that this was all to the good
since it was too late, anyhow, for any useful swotting.
When he was not at the vicarage helping Tamzin with
her letters, or down on the shore swimming with Simo
he was working at the little carved dolphin he was making
for Tamzin from a piece of fallen holly-branch. Burma
sat watching the tiny curls of white wood falling from the
knife, until one fell that especially appealed to him for his
collection, and then he padded away with it sprouting
from the corner of his mouth like a wayward tooth.

On the Saturday morning at the end of this week
Meryon took the little dolphin in his pocket to Westling.
Petrol for the *Emma*'s powerful engine could only be
managed occasionally, with so many other drains on his
pocket money, but there was always his bicycle. And just
as well, too, he said to himself as he turned into the
Westling road and saw the week-end dolphin traffic
already raising the July dust: there would have been no

convenient place to park a full-sized hearse, unless he'd decided to block the vicarage drive with her. He only hoped old Jim would be able to keep Skylark from any car-savaging bouts; there could seldom have been more at hoof, so to speak, to savage.

It was all rather hectic, this living at the centre of a tourist attraction, but he was glad that Tamzin had become reconciled to the idea of sharing Simo. One couldn't help but rejoice at the good fortune that the dolphin had brought to the village. People in Westling were saying that if she stayed the summer through with them they would be able to save enough to make up for years of struggle and adversity. Besides all this, one simply had to admit the astonishing feeling of goodwill and good fellowship that had spread among all the thousands who had now made the journey to see her. Not only had the inns been crowded; so had Mr. Grey's little church. In a world that always seemed to be rattling swords and talking about war, these things were impressive to a young generation who felt that its only hope was in learning to live at peace.

Meryon found Tamzin filling up the ponies' hay-nets in the stable-loft; the long heat-wave had dried up the grass of the little paddock.

"Open your hands and shut your eyes," he was just going to say, but didn't: her eyes when she looked up were troubled; the carving could wait. "What's up?"

She said, "I think Simo's in danger."

"What kind of danger?"

"Not what any of us thought of." She sat on the opened hay-bale, her long legs stuck out at each side of the net, her face anxious and worried. "We thought of people frightening her, or even some crazy shooter taking potshots at her, or trying to harpoon her; but none of us thought of a water circus."

He came and sat with her, pushing hay into the net without paying attention to it. "How d'you know? What do they want to do with her?"

"Oh, I didn't have to do any finding out; it's all quite above-board—so far. They came here; at least, the manager did. He's only just gone."

"What's a water circus, anyway?"

"It's a kind of big swimming pool, he says. They have them in America, and this one is opening somewhere near Hythe at the beginning of August. Aqua-circus, he called it. It has tiers of seats round, and all the stunts they do are water ones; swimming and diving, and so on. They've got some sea-lions and a diving dog."

"I see, and now they think they'd like Simo."

She nodded miserably. "He—Mr. Barrett—asked me if I'd help them to net her. I suppose he saw what I thought because he went on to say how much better off she'd be with the circus; being fed and looked after and so on, and safe from enemies. I said she didn't have any enemies, except people who wanted to capture her."

"You did? Good for you."

"But he isn't the sort of man who would take much notice of anyone saying things like that; he's a super big business man; you know the kind."

"I know. Like a hard-centred chocolate. When you bite them you only hurt your teeth." He rammed the hay down into the nets and dropped them through the man-hole. He and Tamzin followed down the ladder and went out to the paddock, swinging a net each.

She said, "There was a lot more I was bursting to say, such as finding your own food in freedom being better than any luxuries in captivity, whatever kind of creature you are. But I knew it wouldn't be any use. He was only thinking of the money she would bring in. The next thing he said was they hoped I would appear in the circus with her, as the Dolphin Girl, because she would do more for me than for anyone else."

"And because you're in the news, no doubt."

"He said they'd pay very well, and I wouldn't have much to do."

"What did your mother and father say?"

"Oh, nothing very much. You know them, how they always feel they mustn't interfere in other people's lives, even their own children's, unless they're asked."

"Well, I suppose you asked them? What they have to say is usually worth listening to."

"After I'd told Mr. Barrett I couldn't help in any way at all, and he had gone, I asked them. They just said they thought I was right. But Father added he didn't think that that would be the last of it."

"Neither do I. Anyone can fish in the sea."

"That's what Father said."

"Your not helping them doesn't mean they won't have a go at catching her without you. And then showing her without you. After all, she does play with other people, if not as much as with you." He pushed open the paddock gate and the two ponies came trotting, nostrils fluttering, at the sight of the tightly packed hay-nets. Meryon and Tamzin tied the nets on a branch of the silver plane tree where they hung like great tawny tropical fruits under the heavy summer foliage. Cascade took a snatch at the hay and turned, crunching it, to rub the flies off his face on Tamzin's yellow shirt. But Banner just went on eating. He never forgot the lean years when he had lived with the diddikai gipsies.

"What are we going to do?" she appealed to Meryon over Cascade's mane.

"What can we do?" He looked back at her, wishing he were St. George, or the Prime Minister, or even Neptune. "We'll think of something." Remembering the little carved dolphin he took it from his pocket and put it on Cascade's smooth back. It was in a leaping attitude sleek and curving. On Cascade's rounded whiteness it was a dolphin on a crested wave. Tamzin closed her hand over it, smiling her delight.

"It's Simo! It's just the way she jumps." She didn't exactly say thank you, but the way she looked at him made Meryon feel a little giddy.

"I suppose you couldn't look at me like that again, just for another second?"

"I don't know how I did look." Her absolute simplicity was one of the things he loved most about her. She had no affectation.

"In some ways that's a pity; but in others it's what makes you you. I like the way you don't know how you look."

She said, "High water's at half past twelve. Let's swim before lunch."

They went on the ponies. Tamzin was able to take Banner because Diccon and Butterbeans were in charge of Skylark while old Jim traded from the cart. Meryon rode Cascade. He was an indifferent rider, considering that he was so able in most outdoor activities, but he managed. They rode bareback, for the freedom and quickness of it.

Already the long familiar trail was winding down the sea wall to the beach. The donkey-cart was in the thick of it; too wide for the sea wall path, it followed the sheep-tracks that zig-zagged over the close-bitten turf with its outcrops of shingle. The ferryman had bought a barrel of ice-cream to go with his drinks and chocolate, and in the heat of midday was already serving it to tired and dusty families as they trudged along. All the tiny late foxgloves that Tamzin had so much admired were trampled now; the sheep had retreated from the saltings and the curlews had gone. No swans sailed on the Ballast Hole that was reputed to be bottomless. Only the seagulls still whirled and swooped in the sky, learning already that crowds meant hunks of sandwiches.

With the advantage of the ponies Tamzin and Meryon took a wider circuit by the Redshanks' Pool, where they found the swans floating brilliant against the dark sea-coloured water. The redshanks themselves had gone up at the sudden appearance of the ponies and riders crying their warning triple call that was like a ringing of bells. They were forever alert, sentinels for the less watchful birds; but Tamzin knew that as soon as the ponies had passed they would be down again, bobbing and dipping on their long red legs and wading belly-deep.

Coming out to the shore from the quiet Marsh was a sudden sharp contrast.

"You can hardly see the yellow of the shingle between the people," Tamzin said as little Banner muscled into the loose pebbles head down, his hoofs sinking at each step. She swung herself off his back and trudged beside him, as Meryon had done for Cascade. And immediately the people came closing round them again, as they always did, clamouring with their news and their questions.

"We saw you on the telly last night."

"We've all been waiting for you."

"She came once and played a bit, but then she went away again. She'll come back as soon as you're there."

"May we give your ponies these sandwiches? Can we hold them for you? We'll look after your clothes."

"There's a man here wants to put her in a water circus. Did you know?"

Tamzin swung round. "Here? Where?"

"Over there; look!" The child pointed.

Gazing over the heads of Simo's many fans Tamzin recognised Mr. Barrett. Tall and lean, a little stooped and very fair, he was easy to pick out.

"Perhaps he's only watching," Meryon said to her. "In any case, I don't see what we can do about him. Come on and find Simo."

CHAPTER XII

So much Red Tape

SIMO was in wonderful form that morning. As soon as Tamzin was in the sea she was there, leaping and rolling. She had a new game, playing with empty lemonade bottles that people had given her from old Jim's donkey-cart. One or two people even gave her full ones, thinking the empties unworthy of her estimation. She devised a way of pushing the bottles with her snout and at once began racing off with them, one at a time, to a place about fifty yards off-shore, where she left them floating and clinking together, glinting in the sunlight. She always took the full ones first because they were easier to push, but her delighted audience thought otherwise.

"Look! She's taking them out to her mate! She wants him to have a good swig; look at her picking the full ones. Isn't she sweet?"

Tamzin watched her with grief and joy, knowing that Mr. Barrett, too, was watching. It was ironic that Simo should be so much at her best to-day, in front of him, when Tamzin would have been happier even to see her sulk and refuse to play at all.

Now the second dolphin was visible, surfacing in rhythmical, graceful arcs for air. He took no notice at all of the island of bottles that Simo had taken out to him. Tamzin felt a sudden foolish heartache for her dolphin, as for someone whose loving gift has been ignored; but Simo's gaiety was above such disappointments. She began another new and delightful game which consisted of rushing towards some unsuspecting bather at terrific speed and then suddenly stopping dead a foot or so away.

Meryon laughed, swimming slowly past Tamzin who stood watching, swaying to the movement of the waves. "Personal demonstration of dolphin non-turbulent braking power. The next people we'll have here will be the scientists who're interested in how they do it."

"If only she wouldn't do *every*thing in front of that man!" Tamzin exclaimed despairingly.

Late that afternoon Mr. Barrett called again at Westling Vicarage. Tamzin and Meryon were spreading out their towels on the lawn to dry when they saw him. They stood up and answered his greeting. He had come, he said, to ask Tamzin once more whether she wouldn't change her mind.

Knowing that Tamzin very seldom changed her mind, Meryon was astonished to see her hesitate, and then to hear her say after a moment's anxious frowning, "I don't really feel at all happy about it, still. I suppose I just *might* think differently, presently; but I've always hated the idea of animals in cages."

Seeing, like a distant light, a flicker of success at last, Mr. Barrett followed up his advantage quickly and shrewdly. "Well, I'm glad to hear you've been thinking it over; very glad. And as to animals in cages; they're often happier that way, believe me." His blue eyes were not unkind; he really did believe that Simo would be better off in a tank. "You keep a pony in a stable, yourself."

"But that's different. Simo is a wild animal."

He said, "I think if we could just discuss the matter for a few minutes, you would see my point. It would be such a pity, both for you and for us, not to take what might be a wonderful chance for you."

Late arriving trippers who had been hoping for at least a glimpse of the Dolphin Girl, if not of Simo, now paused outside the garden wall telling each other that this must be she, and stood gazing at her. Tamzin and Meryon never noticed them. The village was always crowded these days.

"I—I should have to have more time—I can't say, now."

Meryon stared at her, disbelieving his ears. She didn't look at him but her smoky eyes held their own, with an effort, against the searching glance of Mr. Barrett.

"Well, yes, of course; but there isn't very much time, you know. August is nearly on us, and naturally we're very anxious to have her settled into the tank before the holiday season begins." He had fair lashes as well as fair hair, which surprised Tamzin in the absurd way such things do strike one in a crisis. She was fair herself but her lashes were quite black, which surprised Mr. Barrett.

"How long?" she suddenly asked.

His Adam's apple went up and down when he swallowed, she noticed. He spread his hands. "Perhaps a day or two?"

"Yes, all right, I'll try to make up my mind as quickly as I can; but it might be as long as all that."

Meryon felt that something was slipping from under his feet. After all the years of thinking that he knew and understood Tamzin, now suddenly he was adrift. He could hardly help saying something, before she committed herself further. He said to Mr. Barrett: "The loss of the dolphin would mean a lot to the whole of this village. I expect Tamzin is thinking of that, as well. The people here have never been so prosperous in their lives."

Mr. Barrett turned to Meryon. "You wouldn't say

they're exploiting the dolphin commercially, I suppose?"
The question sounded innocent.

"No, I don't think so. I think their good fortune is just
a result of her being in the bay, of her own free will."

"Put it that way if you like, of course."

"I have," said Meryon, his square chin looking squarer.

"I'll give you my card," Mr. Barrett said to Tamzin,
opening his wallet. "You can get in touch with me quite
quickly, if I'm out of the village; personal telephone call,
reversed charge; they would find me at once."

"Thank you." She took it and stared at it for a moment.

"Well, we shall be seeing each other again fairly soon,
I hope."

She nodded, and courteously he took his leave, his town
shoes slithering on the shingle drive.

Meryon's hands came down on Tamzin's shoulders and
swung her round to face him. "Well?"

"Well what?" She could square her own chin. "You
don't think I meant it, do you?"

"You always have meant what you've said."

"Well, this time I didn't. Don't you realise we've got
to have *time*? If I'd said no, straight away, what d'you
think he'd have done? Gone right off and made arrange-
ments to catch her without me."

Meryon concealed his burst of admiration and said,
"You witch!" looking at her gravely.

Suddenly her voice became urgent. "We've got to think
very quickly, now, what to do. We may only have a
couple of days, unless I can hold him off for longer."

"We could have a family conclave," he suggested. "In
fact, I think we ought to."

Mr. and Mrs. Grey were shelling peas together in the
sun-warmed stable-yard, the one place not overlooked
from the road or shingle.

"Mr. Barrett's been again. I didn't say yes or no

because we've got to have time." Tamzin threw herself into a deck-chair. "We've got to do something to protect Simo."

Helping with the pea-shelling, Meryon even in a crisis was inspecting a maggot with his habitual biologist's eye.

"Well, lovey, if we can," her mother said reasonably, not wishing for Tamzin to fling herself at the impossible. "How had you thought? If you have thought."

"But how can I, all by myself? I want us all to think! It's Simo's only hope."

They all sat thinking; though it did occur to all of them that usually she was the one to have ideas, with everyone else drawn in to act on them.

Meryon suddenly said, popping a pea-shell: "Well, blow me, I don't know why none of us thought of it before, but two dolphins have already been protected by Order in Council; we've all known that for weeks."

The others looked at him. Then Tamzin turned quickly to her father. "Do you think we could?" Suddenly she was full of hope and enthusiasm. "How does one apply for an Order in Council? Is it an Act of Parliament?"

The vicar looked thoughtful. "No. It doesn't go through Parliament. It would all depend on two things; whether there is an existing law on which an Order in Council could be based, and whether the Minister concerned was willing to put it through. It has to be signed by the Sovereign, of course. Or the Governor, I expect, in the case of the New Zealand dolphins."

Tamzin's hand was on his knee. "How long would it take? How long would you say we might have, before they try to get Simo?"

"My dear, they could try for Simo to-morrow, for all we know. An Order in Council could take weeks; if we did succeed in getting one through, which I must say I think is doubtful."

She gazed at him despairingly, already trying to think of alternatives.

Mrs. Grey said, "But surely some temporary protection could be arranged, while the Order was going through. Or what use would such a thing ever be in an emergency?"

Meryon threw the last empty pea-pod into the basket and looked up. "You know what the social reformers always say: write to your M.P."

"But there isn't *time*!" Tamzin cried.

"I could phone him," her father said. "Providing he's at home."

The next minute they were all making for the house, Meryon with the basket and Tamzin clutching the bowl of green peas. They sat in silence while Mr. Grey put through his call, Tamzin and Meryon on the stairs and Mrs. Grey in the sitting-room with the door standing open. The Member was at home. In view of this, Tamzin was disappointed at the briefness of the call. She had expected a lengthy discussion of the problem of ways and means. Her father seemed to do most of the talking and he certainly put Simo's case well.

"What do we have to do, Dad? Does he think it will work, the way it did in New Zealand?" She came jumping off the stairs and across the hall; she was barefooted and in jeans as usual at home in the summer.

"He doesn't know; we can't expect any M.P. to have every law at his fingertips. But he's going to find out."

"Oh, Dad! So much red tape; and all the time Simo is in danger."

"We're lucky, really; he's going up to London on Monday and says he'll make inquiries then, and ring us in the evening. No one could be quicker than that."

"Oh, but they could! It could all be done in a few

hours, if only people understood how urgent it was; if all the right people telephoned each other at once—why not? People get so stolid and plodding. I'll never get stolid when I grow up!"

"Signed, Tamzin Grey!" said her mother, smiling at her. "We could show it to you when you're middle-aged."

Her father said, "Sometimes it might be a mistake to rush through laws and orders. It's really a safeguard for everyone when things take their proper course. Otherwise you might find some enthusiastic Minister suddenly banning all bathing between the hours of sunset and sunrise, say, just because someone once nearly got drowned at it!" He went into his study and stood staring down at his desk. It was Saturday evening, Tamzin remembered, when all of them always tried not to disturb the work of creating sermons. Her mother took the peas into the kitchen. The vicarage cats wandered through after her, gazing at Tamzin and Meryon silent in the hall. The sun shone across the open front doorway, white-hot and shimmering; the crowds had begun to trickle away; cars were starting up in the village street.

"Old Jim would know what to do," Tamzin suddenly said. "I'm practically certain he would."

"I thought you were hardly on speaking terms, after his making money out of your crowds?"

"Oh, that." She dismissed it. "Simo is more important." She had fished the little carved dolphin out of her pocket and stood staring at it, then suddenly she looked up. "Let's go round and find him!"

Meryon glanced at his watch. "Just after opening time; he'll be in the pub."

CHAPTER XIII

To-morrow may be too late

STANDING at the open door of the William the Conqueror, Meryon was surprised and uneasy to see not only Hookey Galley but Mr. Barrett as well, leaning on the counter with old Jim. It was not possible to mistake any of their back views, even across a crowded bar. He withdrew at once to discuss this ominous development with Tamzin, who was waiting at the ferry-hut, playing with the ferry-cat's three kittens. Hookey was a man who seemed to have been born with a grudge against the world. So had his father and grandfather, the village said; and probably also his great-grandfather, the original Hookey who had lost an arm to a shark and so started the family nickname. In nearly all of Tamzin's and Meryon's earlier enterprises they had somehow had Hookey against them. Most of the things they wanted to protect or encourage, it seemed, he wanted to exploit or suppress; and he was a completely ruthless adversary.

Tamzin looked at Meryon anxiously when he told her. "I don't know why I never thought of it. It's just the kind of thing that would attract Hookey; a combination of money-making and doing the other side down."

"He would seem to be just Mr. Barrett's man," Meryon agreed. "Someone who would know exactly how to net a dolphin and probably provide the boat and tackle, and not have scruples about anyone else's feelings."

"Now I come to think of it," she said, "he did go

down to the beach one evening. I thought it was just curiosity; nearly everyone else in the village must have been, except Smiling Morn."

"I expect it was just curiosity. Most likely he never thought that money could be made out of Simo until Mr. Barrett mentioned that he wanted to catch her."

"Jim is the one who surprises me." She looked over her shoulder to the inn, from which cheerful noises of singing were emerging. "I can't think that he could really be bought by the enemy, even if he did turn the crowds to profit. We've had such good times with him for so many years, and he's never let us down."

"It might be a good thing to lure him out of the enemy's clutches, all the same," Meryon suggested. "When you're positively down to each day's earnings, money takes a lot of resisting. Which makes one wonder," he added thoughtfully, "if we have really any right to try to stop him."

Greatly shocked, Tamzin disagreed hotly. "You don't honestly mean you think a few pounds for Jim more important than Simo's freedom? In any case, he must be making quite a bit already, with his donkey-cart trading. Besides, he needn't listen to us if he doesn't want to."

They sat in silence for a minute, gazing at the little harbour crowded with idle fishing-boats: it was far more profitable these days to attend to the many needs of the dolphin pilgrims, than to go out fishing in an over-fished sea. Black river-mud was exposed by the departing tide. It sent up a rich heady smell, assailing their noses. Dunlins ran about on it lightly, where Tamzin would have sunk above her ankles.

Meryon got up from the ferry-hut bench. "I'll see if I can decoy the old chap out."

When he returned some minutes later Hookey was with him as well as Jim Decks. Tamzin saw this with foreboding. It was astonishing that Jim and Meryon had not succeeded in throwing him off. How could they possibly discuss the deliverance of Simo with Hookey there? She looked at them anxiously as they approached

but could tell nothing from their faces. Not one of the three was given to showing his feelings.

"We-ell, gal," Jim said by way of greeting and sat down on the bench.

Hookey lowered himself on to an upturned dinghy that young Jimmy was repairing in the intervals of rowing people over the ferry. He seldom greeted anyone and now uttered a grunt in Tamzin's direction. This was an exceptionally civil thing from Hookey, and she looked at him in wonder while saying hallo, herself.

Meryon straddled the end of the bench. "Jim thinks we may have less than a day. From what he says I should say you didn't really bamboozle Mr. Barrett very much."

Dismay settled coldly somewhere down in Tamzin's chest. Less than a day!

The ferryman nodded. "Looking fer chaps to start in pretty immediate, so he been giving out in the Conk. No one wunt help him, though, not from Westling, stands to reason. He been and tried several, includiating Hookey and me. Don't mind what he pays, neether, seemingly."

"Oh, Jim!"

"'Course, he'll git someone somewheres, choose how. There's plenty up and down the coast as will do any liddle ole job fer money. We-ell, seemed to me *you'd* soon be wanting help smartish, gal." He looked round at her sideways, a little sheepishly, bearing in mind the donkey-cart affair. "And sure enough, in come Meryon. We-ell, we brung Hookey too, as I lay we be glad of him before the night's out."

Tamzin's astonishment grew. The idea of anyone's being glad of Hookey.

"'Course I know he's a lamentable uncivil bloke," Jim acknowledged, as though Hookey were nowhere in ear-shot, "but I sooner have him nor anyone in a proper ole fix, allowing he got his heart in it."

Tamzin considered the idea of Hookey's having a heart in the sense that most people had one. Hookey himself just gazed at the Harbour Mast in his inscrutable way and offered no comment, so Jim went on, "He got his heart in dolphins, see, so that suit us fine. Uncommon fond of dolphins, is Hookey—ancher, Hookey, speak up fer yerself, you gawping ole codfish—always was."

Hookey inclined his head, gazing with silent disdain into the distance. He had the look of a rather treacherous camel, Meryon thought; but he remembered the one time when Hookey had been on their side, and how valuable his ruthless all-or-nothing methods had been.

"He wunt tell you hisself," said Jim, "he wunt tell not no one, but it's all on account of he got mixed up with a dolphin once, time he were a lad."

"Whatever we do," said Meryon, "we've got to do to-night. To-morrow may be too late."

Everyone looked at Tamzin. She was the one who had ideas. "Well, mate," the ferryman said to her, "what you got in mind?"

She spread her hands helplessly. "I only know that we've got to protect Simo, somehow, until the Order in Council is through—if only it does come through. I thought we'd all think of something together."

For all that anyone knew, Hookey was thinking already. He sat delicately picking his teeth with a jack-knife, his angled face giving away nothing. Tamzin jumped at the first stray notion her brain sent up. "We could net her, ourselves, of course; could we take her right out to sea? Perhaps tow her in the net behind *Thunderer* or *Kittiwake*? Then let her loose down the Channel, somewhere."

"I thought you knowed dolphins, gal. That wouldn't be no manner er use—would that, Hookey? 'Course it wouldn't; well, say so, then—and fer why? Fer the reason that she'd up and belt right back to Westling, and in lesser time nor what we'd make it ourselves. Allowing that she didden just escort the ole *Thunderer* home, same as that Pelorus Jack."

"Yes, I suppose you're right." She sighed, frowning with the effort of thought. The piano in The Conqueror across the road behind them began beating out "What Shall we do with a Drunken Sailor?"

"You can't hide her in your bath, mate? No, I lay thass too small."

"Need all of twenny pound of fish a day," Hookey said darkly, and then clamped his mouth shut as if regretting having uttered.

"If we wrote out an Order of our own and put it up, saying that dolphins are protected in the bay until further notice, d'you think the circus people would be taken in?" Tamzin suggested eagerly.

"No." Meryon sounded emphatic. "We'd never be able to make it look official, in the time. It ought to be printed, and no printing works would be open until Monday. There's probably a pretty heavy penalty for putting up unauthorised notices, too."

"Oh, what does that matter?" she cried impatiently.

"I lay we gotter hide her somewheres, thass what," said old Jim, as if dolphins were thimbles.

Seeing some sense in this, for all the difficulties, Meryon began thinking about hiding-places. Suddenly he remembered the swans. They had gone into hiding from the crowds, and he and Tamzin had found the place where they had hidden. He remembered how white they had looked against the dark water. "What about the Redshanks' Pool? It's a fairish distance from the beach, but it's as large as a lake and I'm pretty sure it's sea water; or salt, anyway. No one ever goes that way except sheep and shepherds. In fact, only Castle Farm sheep and Mr. Tewmell. We could warn him."

"Now that really might be the place!" Tamzin had swung round, studying the men's faces. Jim and Hookey nodded slowly, considering the workability of this plan.

Meryon said, "I think we ought to make sure about how salt it is." He looked at his watch. "If you can give me a small bottle I could bike out there and get a sample,

then home through Castle Farm. I've got a bunsen-burner
rigged up in my room. I can get back here quickly in the
Emma."

Tamzin nodded eagerly.

"There isn't any outlet to the sea, of course," he added.
"I don't know how we'd get her there."

"Twenny pound of fish a day," Hookey repeated,
staring at his jack-knife; but no one took any notice.
They would overcome the feeding problem when they
got to it.

"No access for a boat," Meryon said, "too far to carry
her, no road for the *Emma*. The tracks and sheep-gates
aren't even wide enough for Cascade's trap. We tried it,
one summer."

Hookey slid a glance of inspiration round to Jim.
"There's your liddle ole donkey-cart."

"Will that go through past the Redshanks' Pool?"
Meryon thought this unlikely but just possible. Hope
began to flicker and rise.

Jim and Hookey both nodded. "Surely, we been
through more'n one night, ent us, Hookey?" Hookey
glared at him, not answering, but they were safe enough.
In the circumstances, neither Tamzin nor Meryon would
have dreamed of inquiring what they were doing out
there with the donkey-cart at night. Both of them knew,
in any case, that smuggling was in the Westling people's
blood, and in the ferryman's more than anyone else's.
The path by the Redshanks' Pool was the loneliest way to
the shore. It was, moreover, reputed to be haunted by a
ghost called Seaborn Sarah, and so was avoided by all but
the toughest after dark. But Sarah would hurt no one,
Tamzin knew. She was the protecting spirit of Castle
Farm.

"How shall we do it? Is the cart big enough, d'you
think? I suppose we'd have to fit a water-tank inside it?"

"'Course we wouldn't," said old Jim. "You only got to keep a dolphin wet. Now, look here, young 'uns, this is how we do it."

They leaned forward, carefully listening. The sun, dropping lower, sank out of sight behind a rising rampart of thundercloud.

CHAPTER XIV

The Dolphin Catchers

RISSA and Roger bicycled down to Westling late that evening in response to telephone calls from Tamzin. They had been intending to come on the Sunday in any case, and now simply shoved pyjamas and toothbrushes into their saddlebags. Rissa had her usual trouble in getting permission to take part in anything so unusual—or downright dangerous, as it seemed to her urban-minded parents; but she was a very determined person and wore them down on the grounds that everyone else would be allowed to go, and she would only be pitied if she weren't.

Tamzin's parents had fairly easily been persuaded to agree to the midnight dolphin-netting, but they began to be uneasy as the sky grew more threatening from the west. The wind dropped to a hot sultry breath under blackening cloud as Meryon set off on his bicycle. Such trippers as had intended to sleep out on the beach changed their minds, and began the journey home.

"Which couldn't be better from our point of view," Tamzin said at supper. "We don't want anyone on the beach."

Old Jim knew that a considerable storm was boiling up, but he made light of it when Mrs. Grey anxiously asked him. "Oh, ar, I'll lay we git a drop," he admitted casually. He didn't mind weather, himself, except as a driver away of fish and ferry customers. People took too much notice of it; sissy, that was. The vicar, too, was enough of a seaman to know what was coming; but he believed in letting the young be adventurous, unless life or limb were threatened; and what was a thunderstorm but a spectacular noisy wetting? And to-night it wasn't even windy or cold.

High water was at half past midnight. Meryon was back in the *Emma* before dusk with a favourable report on the salinity of the Redshanks' Pool. The filtering through shingle had diluted it a little, but it was still not far below sea-water. They began going over details.

"For the plan to work well," Meryon explained to Rissa and Roger, "Simo must be in the net soon after twelve, so that we can still use the tide to get her ashore. We can't start until after dark, for obvious reasons."

"But won't she die when she's out of water?" Rissa thought of gasping fish on the decks of smacks.

"No, we've only got to keep her wet. We've got an old blanket and a horse-rug, and Hookey's bringing some petrol-tins he uses for water in his smack. Now, listen; you and Roger are to take Skylark and the cart out to the beach, by the lifeboat house, as soon as it's dark. Take the rug and blanket, they're in the hall. The tins will be in the cart. When you get to the beach fill up the cans and soak the blankets in sea-water, and then wait. The rest of us are going round in a herring-boat, the *Jessie*, that Hookey's borrowed. She's got an engine and she's small enough to be handy, and she can trawl for fish on the way."

Heavy drops were beginning to splash on the shingle road when Roger and Rissa went round Smiling Morn's corner. It was dark and no stars shone. The Harbour Mast showed up white against the darkness. Probably the storm-cone had been run up but no one could have seen its dangling, black, canvas dunce-hat. The William the Conqueror had closed but a light showed in its side window. One parked car could be seen where the light fell.

"Mr. Barrett's, I shouldn't wonder," Roger said, having heard the news from Tamzin. "Probably staying at the pub for the night. Let's hope the weather keeps him in."

Skylark was in his little stall, partitioned off in the shed where Jim had kept the *Emma*. He was well bedded down, as Butterbeans and Diccon and the Lillycrop children had left him, eating hay with contented and comfortable noises.

"Pity to disturb him," Rissa said, wedging her torch in a pile of fish-boxes, "but there it is."

The painted cart stood at the other side of the partition, its shafts lifted up like hands in prayer. The torchlight threw stark shaft-shadows high on the wall, and beside those the long exaggerated shadows of Skylark's ears.

The donkey took the bedtime harnessing with a philosophical sigh that Rissa found quite touching. She gave him the whole of the carrot she had in her pocket instead of keeping some for later. Roger was more at home with engines and fumbled over the buckles and traces. When they were outside, shutting the shed door so as to leave no trace of their movements, Skylark suddenly stiffened and shot off towards the inn across the road. The reins were over Rissa's arm, and although she was badly jerked she stopped him, snorting and rigid, a few yards from the car.

"Quaking Queens!" she said, whispering, although the noise had been considerable. "We forgot he goes for cars. What a narrow squeak. I hope they didn't hear in there."

"Making plenty of noise themselves, I expect, with television." But even as he spoke a curtain shook and a face appeared briefly at the window. It was not easy to say whose. Then it had gone and the curtain fell back. "Come on quickly," Roger said. "It's a mercy he didn't do any damage or we might have been held up badly, to say nothing of rousing suspicions."

Mrs. Grey had insisted on raincoats and sou'westers, and they were glad of these as the splashes grew larger.

"What a row the wheels make," Rissa said. "And those tins. Can you pack them round with the rugs a bit better?"

The storm broke when they were passing the martello tower, heading out to the Marsh. In the windless sky it had come up slowly, and slowly it would go. The rain was so static that it was like deep water, through which the donkey and the boy and girl plodded. The thunder made a noise like the end of the world; continuous lightning lit up lines of wild-haired willows.

"I suppose it's rather like war," Roger shouted.

Rissa was having trouble with Skylark, who disliked the noise, the wet and the brightness, all three. She didn't know about Seaborn Sarah, and might have thought her the least of the hazards if she had.

"I wonder about the others, in the *Jessie*," she shouted back, clutching the reins.

"No wind . . . rain'll keep the sea flat . . . shouldn't worry."

The *Jessie* chugged down the swollen river against the tide. She carried two nets, one to catch the dolphin and one to catch fish for the dolphin. Besides Jim and Hookey, Tamzin and Meryon were huddled down, hunched against the rain. Tamzin felt that she was in a world of water, almost as if she might have been a dolphin herself; there seemed so little difference between the water below them and the water around and above. Old Jim steered by the lightning. It was in any case so vivid and continuous that it swamped the beacon lights, as the barrage of thunder drowned the noise of the engine. The rain was blue and shivered, as if it were part of the lightning. When they were out on the rocking water of the bay Tamzin felt sick. She always did feel sick at sea, but now it came on sooner because of fear and worry and excitement. So much had to go right; the fishing, the finding and capture of Simo, and the trek to the Redshanks' Pool.

"Lovely drop er weather," shouted Jim, the rain running off his beard. "Keep everyone minding their own business, so we can mind ourn unprovocated."

"What shall we do if we don't find her?" Tamzin said to Meryon between the crashes. "We've never been near her at this time of night."

"You were, once," said Meryon.

Hookey looked round at them. He had on his particularly ferocious scowl that passed for a smile. "Thass the idea—throw the gal over; that'll fetch the dolphin!"

Tamzin grinned back, but she shuddered a little, leaning closer to Meryon.

In a minute she was helping to shoot the trawl. Jim at the tiller shouted at them all, but half his words were lost in the tumult. He looked like the Flying Dutchman, Tamzin thought, as he stood there driving the little boat on into the storm.

Coming near to the Redshanks' Pool, Skylark suddenly stopped still and shivered. Rissa, who had gone on plodding, jerked at his mouth before she realised. "Come on!" she said, pulling at the rein, but Skylark leaned back on his haunches. "Hell's bells!" said Rissa. "What's all this?"

"He's shivering," Roger said, resting a hand on the soaking back. "Perhaps he's caught a chill? Anyone easily might."

"Not donkeys. Get on, Skylark! Try giving a shove behind, Roger."

"Behind the donkey, or the cart?"

"Gump," said Rissa.

Shoving behind the cart merely sent the shafts up in the air.

"Anyone'd think he'd seen a ghost," Rissa said disgustedly. "What now? Get in the shafts ourselves? There isn't another track through."

"We could try blindfolding?" Roger hazarded, expecting scorn. Like Meryon, he was not a horsy person.

"Why ever didn't I think of it?" It was obviously the only thing. Roger felt like someone who has drawn a winning number. "Is there anything in the cart we can blindfold with?" she asked.

Roger looked. The rain sluiced down his neck as he bent his head. He could only look during the flashes, but they were nearly incessant. "Nothing but the blankets; and they're one thing we shan't have to soak when we get there." He brought the smallest one, but however they arranged it, it eclipsed the whole donkey, so that he looked like a kind of baby elephant. Rissa made encouraging noises and tugged at the rein, her hand under the blanket. Skylark shot forward obediently and the shaft hit Rissa's leg. What she said was drowned by thunder, and Roger's fleeting grin was hidden in the total dark between two flashes.

"It worked, anyway," she shouted.

"I wonder if he really did see a ghost?" Roger said. "There's supposed to be one, somewhere around here."

The *Jessie* trawled through the storm, pushing westwards across the bay. They hauled in the net when they were opposite the lifeboat house; they had only been dragging for fifteen minutes or so. Tamzin hardly expected anything from so short a fishing, but mackerel

and whiting poured from the net into the boat, metallic in the blue flashes.

"Enough for her mate as well!" Meryon said, piling them into the boxes.

"I forgot her mate," Tamzin suddenly said. "He'll miss her."

"Gotter catch her first, gal." Jim put the tiller over and headed shorewards. "Wonder how Skylark and them are making out?" After a minute he said, "Call your dolphin, young 'un."

"She'll never hear; even when it isn't thundering the rain's like drums." But she called, "Simo! Simo!" wondering if she would have to go into the sea.

"Bin follerin' us these five minutes," Hookey observed: he had seemed to be busy with the engine most of the time.

Tamzin swung round and peered through the rain, astern. "Why didn't you say?" What a cussed character Hookey was.

It was difficult to make out Simo's curving dorsal fin as she broke surface to breathe; there was, most of the time, plenty of light, but the rain was an opaque curtain. Anyway, it was a relief to forget about having to go overboard. "Simo! Here I am!"

"As if she didn't know," Meryon said.

"Fetch her up alongside, gal," said Jim. "We're getten middling close inshore."

They were indeed very close; it was possible to sail ashore at high tide. Rissa and Roger, standing with Skylark at the edge of the sea, saw the whole capture by the light of the storm. They saw Hookey and Meryon holding out the small net with boat-hooks while Tamzin leaned over the side calling Simo. They heard, between thunderclaps, the cry of disappointment as Simo slid straight through the net and escaped them. Then the

Jessie had to jockey round, and out went the net again. No one, aboard or ashore, was really surprised when Tamzin suddenly jumped into the sea. Where the *Jessie* was it was scarcely three feet deep, and very warm, and it was so much easier to help when one was in the water with the dolphin.

Rissa and Roger couldn't help raising a cheer when the net was hauled in. Nobody heard them but it let off their feelings.

"What a storm!" Roger shouted, realising that they hadn't even heard themselves. "Can you remember one going on as long as this, ever before?"

"Here she comes!" said Rissa. "Everything's ready, I think; petrol-tins full, blankets wet."

"I only hope they've caught the right dolphin," Roger said, turning Skylark so that the cart backed on to the sea.

CHAPTER XV

Donkeys Always Know

TAMZIN soon wasn't the only one in the sea. First Meryon and then Hookey went in after her, to help hold the dolphin in the net as they hauled her to the shore. Old Jim drove the *Jessie* at full speed into the shingle and then jumped out, himself. Roger ran down to help him pull the bows aground and pitch the anchor in the beach banks.

"Jus' made it, son. Tide's at the flood; be turning any minute."

The others were struggling through the breakers with Simo. There was now more darkness as the storm lessened a little in intensity. It was still of nearly tropical fierceness, but no longer did one flash seem to link with another.

"We'll never get her into the cart," Rissa said, now seeing the dolphin and cart together for the first time.

"'Course not, mate." Jim and Roger came stumping up with the fish-boxes which they slid into the sides of the donkey-cart. "But we can git her fore end in, then we only got half to carry. I lay she weigh nigh fower hunnerd pound."

Swathing a large, slippery, wet dolphin in wet blankets in a black downpour, and then easing her into the donkey-cart, was nearly a superhuman task, even for five able-bodied people. Rissa had to stay at Skylark's head. Tamzin was tired and distressed. She kept talking to Simo and to anyone else who might hear, as they panted and struggled together. "Simo! It's me. We're trying to save you. . . . Listen! She's making a kind of whistling noise. D'you think she's all right?"

"Of course she is," said Meryon reassuringly.

"To me!" yelled Jim. "To me a little—steady! To you."

"We'll put you back in the sea again as soon as we can!" Tamzin said, but her voice was lost in thunder.

"Gently does it!" yelled Jim.

"Starboard a little!" grunted Hookey.

"My hand's trapped!" Roger called out.

"She's a bit tight this side," warned Meryon.

"It's all right, Simo!" Tamzin called to her. "D'you think she understands, or does she think I'm betraying her?"

The great effort over, they stood in silence getting their breath for a minute. The roar of breakers on the shingle mingled with the relentless roar of rain on the sea. Forked lightning over the bay was spectacular, but this was no time for admiring it. The only comment it drew was from Meryon, as he adjusted his hold on the blanket that supported Simo's tail end.

"Enough electricity let loose to-night to light all London for a year."

Then they were all trudging up the beach banks, heads down, hoofs and shoes sliding. Rissa was at Skylark's bridle, Hookey and Jim and Meryon supporting Simo's projecting tail end, Tamzin and Roger sloshing water from the petrol-tins on to the blankets and the boxes of fish. Everyone's feet were squelching in their shoes, even Rissa's, the only ones that hadn't been in the sea.

"Simo's squelching, too," Tamzin said to Roger. "We might as well save the water in the cans, in case it stops raining."

"Supposing it doesn't stop? I feel like Noah. Perhaps we ought to build an ark."

When they came off the beach banks it was difficult finding the sheep-track, now that the lightning was less frequent. They waited for it, Skylark blowing and heaving in the shafts after the tough pull up the loose shingle. For a minute there was only the sound of the rain, now that the breakers were a hundred yards behind them and the thunder momentarily silenced. Simo was making a creaking noise that sounded like rusty hinges. Tamzin patted her anxiously. Then the sky was split by a triple white charge, and in the light of it they saw the wind-crippled thorn tree that marked the track. Under a crash like the fall of a cathedral they plodded towards it.

"Whew! That was a close one," Tamzin said, trying not to panic.

"I'll bet there've been some houses struck, to-night," Rissa observed briskly, as if trying to look on the bright side. "Have you ever heard of those queer red floating fire-balls that waft in at open doors and wander down passages, and finish up in aluminium saucepans? And there were those mountaineers whose ice-axes started humming in a storm——"

"Shut up, Rissa!" Meryon said sharply, knowing that Tamzin was near enough to being jittery. Another resounding crash silenced her for him.

"Marvellous how everything's going," Roger remarked cheerfully when the racket had subsided.

"That don' do to provocate the gods," said Jim severely.

They trudged on in silence, nearing the Redshanks' Pool. Sometimes, in lightning, they could see where it was, by the line of witches'-broom willows reaching their wild branches to the sky.

Tamzin looked at them, stark against the dazzle. "The

witches have got more than even magic can do, to sweep
this storm away."

And then, when they were nearly there, Skylark suddenly stopped.

"Oh, not again!" cried Rissa. "He did this coming. We
had to blindfold him. It's so silly, because he doesn't take
much notice of the thunder."

"I lay thass ole Sarah," Hookey suddenly exclaimed.
"Donkeys allus knows." There was stark horror in his
usually bellicose voice, to Tamzin's astonishment.

"You mean Seaborn Sarah—of course! I forgot she
walks here on really stormy nights. She was Mr. Merrow's
grandmother, the first Mrs. Merrow at Castle Farm; but
she was born at sea and lived for years in sailing ships.
The Merrows say she comes back to protect the farm on
stormy nights. But she's all right. She never hurts
anyone. We've only got to blindfold Skylark again, and
go on."

"That we never, mate," Jim stated doggedly. Everyone
gazed at him. It wasn't to be believed: that these two
tough brandy-running fishermen, whom no storm, no
sea, no coastguard had ever intimidated, should be afraid
of ghosts.

"But we must go on!" she shouted through thunder.

A flash lit up Hookey's craggy face turned back seawards. In a muttering whisper he was saying something
about seeing to the *Jessie*. Jim's voice was steady enough
but absolutely flat. "Then you goo, gal, but not wid
Hookey and me. Thass flying in the face of nature, ask
any fisherman. An' on a night like this!"

"But it's only on nights like this that she's *there*!"
Tamzin was exasperated. "Do you expect us to go and put
Simo back into the sea, after all that struggle and effort?"

"There's no real reason why we shouldn't go on by
ourselves," Meryon suddenly said, "if Jim and Hookey

want to get the *Jessie* off. We ought to manage; it's only another few yards."

"Ought? Jolly well will!" Rissa shouted from the front. Call themselves seamen, she thought, smugglers, if it came to that—and scared of a ghost that doesn't even exist! Hookey was almost quaking.

"Well, yes," said Roger, "but what are we going to blindfold with? Both the blankets are round Simo."

Meryon freed a hand from holding up Simo and pulled off his sou'wester. "If that's all that's worrying us—I'm so wet, a little more won't make any difference."

Roger passed it along to Rissa, who fiddled for a bit with the tying-strings and then said she thought it would do. Jim and Hookey silently relinquished their corners of the supporting blanket to Roger and Tamzin, their faces expressing horror mixed with disapproval. There was obviously no stopping the four young lunatics, but Jim was not at all sure in his mind about committing a fairly innocent donkey to the whims of outraged spirits. Suspecting this, Tamzin called out firmly to the others, "Ready, ahoy, then! So long, Jim and Hookey! We'll rub Skylark down when we get back."

"Eh, gal, iffen you do git back." He was loath to see them go alone and into such peril, but nothing would have made him go too. Looking into the vivid rain he saw that Hookey was already heading back along the track to the sea. The donkey-cart was on the move again.

Rissa couldn't resist a last shot. "You'd better look out, Jim! If she comes from the sea she'll probably be footing it back there," she called out wickedly.

Jim turned and pounded after Hookey.

"You'd never think he'd been thirty years cox of the lifeboat," she said.

Skylark went willingly enough with Meryon's sou'-wester tied across his blinkers. Meryon's black hair was so tough and kinky that the rain ran off it without affecting it. Rissa noticed in the flashes and felt how unfair it was. Her own hair would never curl or kink; she had given up hope about it, now, and she wasn't the kind to assist it.

Tamzin was anxious about Simo's breathing, trying to listen to it through the roaring hiss of the rain. All the water in the petrol-tins had now been poured over the blankets; there was nothing more anyone could do except reassure with hand and voice; but the trek was nearly at its end.

There were no swans on the Redshanks' Pool, and no feathers floating; only the rain bouncing on the water.

Rissa said over her shoulders as she led Skylark along beside the reeds, "And no ghosts either. Where's the best place to get down?"

"There's only one possible place," Tamzin said, "where the bank drops down, by the gorse."

"We'll have to use our torches, here," Meryon said. "Too tricky without. We don't want to fetch up in the pool with Simo."

With guidance from the others Rissa backed the donkey-cart nearly to the water's edge. In the torchlight the bank was a rich sultana pudding, with pebbles packed closely in the dark marsh soil. Wind-ruffled water lapped against it. Roger noticed and said, "Wind's stirring again; that'll blow away the storm."

"It'll take all four of us to lift her in," Meryon said when the cart had stopped, "one to each blanket-corner. What about Skylark, Rissa? Nothing to tie him to. Will he stand?"

"He always does, unless there's a car in sight."

"Well, that's hardly likely. In any case he's blind-folded."

She came down the bank and took a tail corner from

D.S.   I

Roger. Tamzin had the other. Meryon took the top rug off the dolphin, then he and Roger stood on the wheel-hubs and leaned over to lift the front of the under-blanket. Meryon's torch was stuck into the bank. Free of Rissa's restraining hand Skylark sighed and shook himself in the shafts. The whole cart trembled and water flew off his thick coat to mingle with the rain.

"Ready? Lift!" Meryon said.

They moved the dolphin six inches.

"Ready again? Lift!"

Another six inches.

"She's making her creaking noise again," Tamzin said anxiously. "Do you think we're hurting her?"

"What else can we do than what we're doing?" Rissa demanded. "We can't have second thoughts now."

"Ready?" came Meryon's voice. "Lift!"

When Simo was at last free of the cart they stood breathing hard in the torchlit rain, clutching the sodden blanket which hung heavy from their hands. Simo made no effort to struggle, as if understanding the folly of doing so. Everyone looked at Meryon. He said, "Nothing for it but going into the pool ourselves, till it's deep enough for her to swim."

"It doesn't matter," Tamzin said, "we're all so wet already."

They shuffled down into the water. The low torch sent their shadows darting out across the pool, blacker than the dark water. Rissa slipped on the mud of the bottom and collected herself violently, but too late to stop Simo slithering out of the blanket into water too shallow for her to swim. They had to gather her up and somehow haul her, between them: Tamzin winced at every move and said that they were hurting her.

"Oh, shut *up*," Rissa said impatiently, "you only make everything more difficult." She was very wet, and shaken by her slip, and not too sure about Skylark left standing by himself.

Suddenly Simo streaked out of their hands and dived; the depth of the pool plunged very steeply; it had been made by removing shingle for ships' ballast in earlier times.

"Now the fish," said Rissa, though everyone else still stood in the water, staring into the small area of wet torchlit darkness and waiting eagerly for a flash of lightning.

Looking back over her shoulder, Tamzin splashed out with the others to help with the boxes of fish. There were two of these, and they were just tipping the fish out into the waters of the pool when there was a quick scrabble of hoofs and a noise of wheels on stones.

Rissa straightened up with a jerk, the water round her knees. "Skylark! He's gone!"

They pounded out again, splashing mud and water, hauling the empty boxes. There was no sign or sound of the donkey-cart, only the bare bank and the noise of rain and thunder.

CHAPTER XVI

Lonely Dolphin in the Bay

IT WAS a long trudge home in the storm and darkness when some of them at least might have been inside Skylark's cart.

"He was rubbing his face on his knee when we were unloading the fish-boxes," Meryon said. "I think he must have dislodged the sou'wester."

"And seen the ghost you mean?" Roger asked. He was interested and a little uneasy, glancing back into the dark behind them.

"How can we know what he saw?" Meryon could never be driven into positive statements about unknown things. He had a seeking mind.

"At least we got the fish out, first," Tamzin said thankfully. "It would've been pretty wretched for Simo, in prison and nothing to eat."

"I'd like to know what Jim's going to say when Skylark bolts home without us," Roger suddenly said.

"He'll never know." Rissa sounded confident. "We'll find Skylark waiting for us outside the stable."

And so they did, though it was not far from dawn when they were trudging, tired and sodden, round the Point. Already there was enough pale watery light to make out the shape of a donkey, standing head down against his stable door and dozing in his shafts. The storm had passed, but could still be heard growling in the distance. Only a little light rain fell on a freshening wind. The dry Marsh had soaked up gratefully its millions of tons of water. Tamzin thought she could almost hear the cottage gardens growing again as she plodded past the fences; certainly you could *smell* them growing, a strong, surging, earthy, leafy smell that made you think of jungles.

Skylark lifted his long ears at the sound of their approach, and his melancholy face visibly brightened. Hay, dry straw and comfort, he was plainly thinking, as anyone could see.

"Really, you know, humans are rather wonderful animals," Roger reflected as they busied themselves with these things; "the way we always see to other animals' comfort before our own. And I'm sure I'm much tireder than Skylark is."

Tamzin looked up, bleary-eyed with tiredness herself. "That's only because we keep them captive. We *owe* it to them. Look what Simo did for me, and not owing me anything."

They let themselves into the vicarage very quietly, but Mrs. Grey heard them. She had been sleeping lightly, listening to the storm and for sounds of their safe return; or for a shout of fear from Diccon if the storm woke him up. He didn't mind thunder in the daytime, but at night all things were more fearful. She put on her dressing-gown and tiptoed down. At least she could see that they had hot drinks and a good towelling before they tumbled into bed, the boys in the spare room and Rissa on a camp bed up in Tamzin's attic. And she could make sure that they were all safe and well.

Roger in fact was so hungry, as he often was, that he ate large quantities of sandwiches as well, though the others simply wanted sleep. Mrs. Grey had only a brief account of the night's doings.

"Food," said Meryon thoughtfully, looking at Roger

through the steam from his hot chocolate, "that really is going to be our worry from now on. What did Hookey say a dolphin eats—twenty pounds of fish a day?"

"And nobody fishing, now," said Rissa.

Tamzin roused herself to demolish this obstacle. "We can go fishing ourselves. We can easily manage the *Jessie*."

"Time enough to think of that to-morrow," her mother said, shepherding them all to the stairs.

"It's to-morrow now," said Tamzin. "It's almost broad daylight. Mother, do you believe in ghosts?"

Mrs. Grey laughed, softly so as not to wake Diccon. "That's a complicated question for anyone to answer in one minute. Ask me another time."

The night's heavy storm broke up the July heat-wave. It was much cooler that next day, with the perpetual Marsh wind blowing. Even though it was a Sunday, far fewer people came down the long road to see the dolphin.

Tamzin and Rissa and the boys got up for a late and hasty breakfast. They had had less than five hours' sleep.

"But I don't feel a bit tired; just hungry," Roger said, cutting the bread very thickly.

"You'll feel tired to-morrow," Rissa told him. "It's always the next day it gets you."

Tamzin kept worrying about whether Simo was all right. She wanted to dash straight off on Cascade to see for herself, but her mother said proper breakfasts were to be eaten by everyone, and washing up and ponies done as well.

They were all excused church this morning because Rissa and Roger had not brought any clothes except what they were wearing. Tamzin knew that she would be expected to go in the evening, as the vicar's daughter and a member of the choir. Diccon now went with his mother, wearing an unbearably self-righteous expression; especially, Tamzin said, as he was leaving her to water his pony. He should have done it for himself, but he was preoccupied with a saucer full of sundew plants that he and Butterbeans Pope had found growing in a bog.

"They eat insects," he explained to Rissa and Roger, "they really do. You put a fly on one of their sticky plates, like this, and the sundew closes over it and digests it. The trouble is finding enough insects." He leaned over, watching it in reverent awe, as one of the mysteries of life; but Tamzin was horrified.

"Future eminent biologist at work," Meryon said to her, and she felt suddenly that Meryon was right, and Diccon was right, and a chap must study his subject. But not herself: it was bad enough to inflict distress on a dolphin in the interests of future good.

"Do you believe in doing harm so that good may come?" she suddenly asked her father as he was billowing out of the door in his cassock.

"My good girl, what a question to answer yes or no," he said, much as Mrs. Grey had done. "I'll preach about it to-night, if you like. Remind me later."

"We must see if Simo is all right!" Tamzin said again when he had gone. "How are we going to get there without people seeing? And what about fish for to-night?"

"It's just as important," Meryon said, "for people to think she's still in the bay. If you suddenly stop going——"

"I ought to have gone before breakfast," Tamzin said, "then I could have done both."

Rissa provided a solution. "We've got to divide. Of course Tamzin must go down to the beach as usual, and someone must go to the Redshanks' Pool, and someone must go fishing."

"Jim ought to be persuadable to go fishing," Roger

suggested, "if he can borrow the *Jessie* again: *Thunderer's* far too big to go out for a couple of hours' fishing. Even with *Jessie* he could catch enough in an afternoon to make a donkey-cart load to sell himself, as well as for Simo. He couldn't do much ice-cream and drinks trade in this weather."

"Bags I be one of the fishers," Rissa said quickly, much preferring this to solitary inland scouting. So did the others. In the end they tossed up, and she lost, and wished they hadn't tossed up. But so it was.

Jim was willing to be persuaded. Moreover, to everyone's relief, he seemed not to have noticed the precipitate arrival home of Skylark the night before.

Tamzin watched the departure of the others and wished she could have changed places with any of them, but particularly with Rissa. Her mind was with Simo all the time. After she had watered the ponies she bridled Cascade and rode down to the sea.

Only a few scattered sightseers were on the sea wall path; perhaps a quarter of the crowds that had been coming. Tamzin was able to ride without constant dodging and slowing down. She could see the *Jessie's* bare mast moving down the river, but no sign of a solitary figure walking on the Marsh. Rissa was a good one for the job of secret agent. She knew nearly as well as Tamzin all the low ground and all the cover available.

Down on the shore were more people than Tamzin had expected, and among them was Mr. Barrett. He came straight up when he saw her on Cascade, appearing still to believe in her new attitude, for all that she knew he had been planning the capture without her. We're deceiving each other, that's what, she said to herself, and he's no more taken in than I am. But we keep it up because he thinks I might come round, and I think I might gain time.

"We've seen her several times this morning," he told Tamzin.

She stared at him in amazement, but happily he had just turned to look at the sea and didn't notice as he went on, "but she isn't coming in as she usually does. Perhaps something's frightened her. Look, there she is; she hasn't been any closer than that."

As soon as she looked Tamzin knew that of course it was Simo's mate. She was not good at deception and was in dire fear of discovery, but now she composed her expression and said, "It was a terrific storm last night. Do you think it could have been that?"

"Possibly, possibly." He looked up at her. "Going swimming? She may come for you."

Tamzin's mind scrabbled over this simple question in a frantic few seconds. If I do, and he sees the dolphin doesn't come, what? And if I don't, will he suspect I know it isn't Simo? She said casually, "Not yet; I got up late and I've only just had a huge breakfast. High water's about two o'clock."

"Just after lunch! Or is everything late on a Sunday?"

Tamzin had a sudden fresh horror that he would wonder why she had got up late, but he only said, "Had any more thoughts about my offer?"

"I—I'm still thinking about it," she said, wishing she had taken more interest in school drama; how *did* you act what you weren't feeling? "I really will let you know in a day or two."

"I can't promise that a day or two mightn't be too late; but I'd much rather work with you than against you: for the dolphin's sake as well as yours. She's going to miss you, you know, if you don't come in with us. You must think of that."

She nodded, troubled and anxious—still more than a day before they could hear about the Order in Council—

but people from the crowd came pressing up to Cascade to talk to her.

"Are you going in? She'll come if you go in."

"She's just staying far out, to-day."

"We've thrown balls and rings and bottles, but she won't take any notice. Everyone's so disappointed."

As soon as she could Tamzin rode home.

Her family was back from church and Diccon was busy with tweezers and a match-box among the vicar's roses when she rode past.

"I'm just going to try aphids on my sundews," he told her, glancing up briefly. "They suck sap," he explained kindly. "It ought to be interesting to see what happens."

"I wonder who'll win, the aphids or the sundews?" she said, trying to get her mind off Simo.

"The sundews, of course."

"Then you know already what will happen."

"But it's still interesting," he said, looking at her pityingly, as at one who would never have a mind for natural sciences. One wild dolphin was all the natural science that Tamzin felt she could cope with at present, and she rode on round to the stable-yard.

The boys had taken sandwiches but Rissa arrived back in time for one o'clock lunch at the vicarage.

"Was she all right? Did you see her?"

Rissa nodded. "Of course the redshanks all went up, jingling like mad, and I thought they'd give me away, but it was all right. I had to wait nearly fifteen minutes; it's incredible how long dolphins can stay under; then she came up to breathe. Just up and down again. I didn't stay much longer in case someone saw, but I think she's all right. Our petrol-tins were strewn all along the track, of course. We never thought of that, last night. I hid them in the gorse. We can pick them up when we're coming back with the empty cart, after dark."

A great relief surged through Tamzin. She hardly knew, herself, how anxious she had been about Simo; whether she had been hurt at all on the journey, whether the pool suited her and how she was getting on.

"Has she been eating, d'you think?"

"There weren't any fish floating. But I don't see how we can be sure she's eaten them."

Tamzin nodded. "Her mate's in the bay. The people think it's Simo. I *think* Mr. Barrett thought it was her, too, but I can never feel certain with him. Sooner or later I've got to go swimming again, and then he'll guess; I'm sure he will."

"We'll think of something," Rissa said. "We always do."

CHAPTER XVII

Dash to the Rescue

IN THE MIDDLE of lunch Hookey Galley came striding down the path to the vicarage back door. Old Jim always came to the front; it was just the difference in the openness of their attitudes. Not that Hookey often came: so seldom, in fact, that Tamzin and Rissa were struck by a sense of disaster as soon as they looked up through the window at the sound of footfalls and saw him. Hurriedly asking permission of Mrs. Grey both of them rushed to the back door.

Hookey said, "Thought I better come, Jim being at sea, but that Barrett he gooing out to the Redshanks' Pool this arternoon."

Tamzin was appalled. "How do you know?"

"He arst Mrs. Gudgeon at the Conk iffen he could use their phone. She got a extension in her kitchen, but she were busy in the bar. I goo round the back and listen-in," he explained simply, as if this were a perfectly honourable thing to do; as indeed it probably was by Hookey's standards.

Tamzin gazed at him, hardly knowing what to think, but Rissa said at once, "What did he say?" She was very down-to-earth.

"He say, is that the Aqua-rarium? I gooing fer the dolphin s'arternoon, git Ron and them out here at once with the tank-truck and gear. Then he give them some directions how to git here, and he say, we can't git the truck through them sheep-gates, put in tools fer lifting fence-posts and knocking 'em back. Then I hear Mrs Gudgeon, the ole basket, coming back and I tunes off and belts it."

"But how could he *know*?" Tamzin could scarcely believe it, but Rissa suddenly remembered the face at the Conqueror's window.

"He *may* have seen us leaving with the donkey-cart; someone did. If it was him he must have wondered, at that time of night and with that storm brewing. Especially after your seeming to change your mind so suddenly. He may even have followed us, for all we know." A fresh thought came to her. "If he did, he could have been the thing that frightened Skylark. But," she added, as the other two seemed struck dumb, "what are we to do now? Jim *would* be at sea, and the boys, too."

The more Tamzin tried to think the more she couldn't. She felt like a person shut in a wardrobe trying to see.

"We could take the donkey-cart out, and see if we can catch her and shift her again," Hookey suggested.

"But where to?" Tamzin cried. "There's only the Ballast Hole, and that's much smaller and so visible, and anyway we'd be seen moving her." She looked from Hookey to Rissa. "If we took a net, and I went into the pool and got the net round her, I'd have caught her, wouldn't I? No one can take a fish out of someone else's net. I'd only have to stay in the pool with her until they went. Or until Jim and the others get back. And to-morrow, too, until we know about the Order in Council, in the evening. Then everything will be all right," she said optimistically, "and we can put her back in the sea."

"But why a net?" said Rissa. "A piece of rope would be enough. You've only got to get it round her and keep hold of the other end. Her flippers and dorsal fin would stop it slipping off."

"I'm going out there at once, on Cascade." Tamzin couldn't waste a moment now that the idea had presented itself. "I must get there before them. How long will they take to get out from Hythe, Hookey?"

"Well, they gotter load up, first; about a hour and a half, I lay."

"You needn't think we're letting you go out there alone," Rissa said. "Anything might happen. Hookey and I'll come along in the donkey-cart." Hookey wouldn't back out, she knew, not because of any concern for Tamzin but because of Simo.

Mrs. Grey, coming into the kitchen to see what was happening, listened to Tamzin's scrambled explanations while Hookey and Rissa went round to harness Skylark.

"But, to go into the water just after lunch, in this cold wind—and you haven't even finished your lunch," she said, almost convinced that this was a time for parental refusal.

"It won't be just after lunch when I get there: I won't even go in until we see the circus people coming. Oh Mother, please see I've *got* to do it!"

Mrs. Grey hesitated, and at once saw that she was lost, as always when she hesitated. But she also saw that Tamzin was right when she said she *had* to do it; and she knew that if Tamzin's father were appealed to, he would agree with Tamzin. She was in half a mind to consult with him, all the same, but it was Sunday, with afternoon and evening sermons ahead of him—he had a second church over the river—and she did not do so. She said, "I've got a spare clothes-line you can borrow if you like. It's strong but light. I'll find it while you saddle up."

The dolphin pilgrimage was gathering in numbers

again when Tamzin rode out of the village with the coiled rope tied to her saddle. She took a devious route behind Harbour Farm, so as not to be seen if possible. There were people in the regular dolphin crowd who would run straight out towards her on sight of the now well-known white pony. Rissa and Hookey in the donkey-cart did provoke some speculating glances as they spanked past the martello tower, especially when they forked on to the sheep-track towards the Marsh, but no one attempted to follow them. Hookey had no more knowledge of horseflesh than sailors usually have, and he had all their suspicion, so Rissa drove. She drove like Jehu, furiously, but there was never any hope of catching Tamzin's half-Arab Cascade.

When they came to the pool the redshanks, which had all gone up for Tamzin and come down again, now all went up for Rissa and Hookey, jingling their alarm call. Cascade was standing underneath a willow, swishing the flies with his tail. A voice came out of the willow branches, "Hallo! I can see farther from here. No sign of Barrett's van, yet, but I've been talking to Simo. She's making much more noise herself than we ever heard in the sea. D'you think she's calling to her mate? Or could she possibly be answering me?"

"How can anyone say?" Rissa was tying Skylark, not too near to Cascade. The donkey seemed now completely unconcerned about the dangers round the pool and began devouring willow-leaves.

Tamzin, jittery as a redshank herself, was peering here and there through the branches. Hookey rolled himself a cigarette and sat on the bank in sombre silence staring at a spider near his feet, though the pool was beautiful with swans and golden gorse before his eyes.

"There she is!" Tamzin suddenly cried. "No, I mean Simo, of course," she exclaimed as Rissa craned her neck to look down the track for a van. "But, oh, look! Look!" Tamzin's voice went up again. "There *is* the van!"

Rissa hardly knew which way her neck was twisting. Quickly she climbed into the willow and saw for herself.

"Yes, I think it must be; but it's a long way off. No need to panic. You can't get down until I do."

"It looks a long way off, but it'll be here in no time, you'll see. My swim-suit's on underneath, but I've got to get my clothes off, and get out to Simo; she isn't coming in very close, even for me. But I'm sure she knows it is me."

Hookey got up and began strolling back down the path. Tamzin supposed this was modesty, though he must have seen hundreds of swimmers in the harbour in his time. Then, with the pressure of mounting emergency, she forgot him. Rissa was frankly pleased not to have him too handy, as long as he was somewhere within call.

With fearful suddenness the van came nearer. Tamzin tore her favourite old faded blue shirt in trying to get it off too fast. Then when they could almost hear the engine, the van came to a stop at the post-and-rail fence.

"That'll hold them up for a bit," said Rissa with satisfaction. But it didn't. The cross-rails were made to take out easily, and lifting a couple of posts was no problem to Mr. Barrett's men. A few good shakes in ground softened by the downpour and out they came. The van moved through. Tamzin was out in the pool now calling her dolphin, the rope coiled over her shoulder. There had been no time to bother with her tied-back hair which floated behind her like a fan. Rissa leaned from the willow branches watching the van come nearer. It came fast, bouncing on the uneven sheep-track. Tamzin was in despair because she could hear the motor, and Simo wouldn't come near her but stayed far out, off one of the pool's two islands. Her curved fin dived and surfaced to the wavelike movement of her swimming.

"She thinks I betrayed her," Tamzin cried to Rissa, full of grief. But Rissa was watching the van. Suddenly it had begun to flounder and now bumped to a stop. Men jumped out and ran round to the back.

"They're changing a wheel!" she shouted to Tamzin. "Oh, glory! I believe they've got a puncture."

Filled with renewed hope, Tamzin put her head down and thrashed on through the water towards the island. "Simo! It's me." Always before the dolphin had raced to meet her.

Good men can change a wheel in less than five minutes. Tamzin was almost near enough to touch Simo when the van came bouncing on again. She was talking to her all the time, not daring to make a quick movement.

Rissa, watching the enemy and vaguely wondering where Hookey was, could hardly believe herself at all when once more the van floundered, swerved, and limped to a stop. The men jumped out and ran this time to a different wheel. Incredulously Rissa called out to Tamzin, "They've punctured *again*. Place must be littered with broken bottles. We'll be really in luck if they haven't another spare." Then she saw Hookey coming back along the brink of the pool with his curious lurching walk, and she wondered.

"They haven't!" she called as soon as she saw repairs in progress. "Oh, what incredible luck!" Scrambling down the tree she made the most of the respite by moving Skylark to a place where he couldn't see the van when it did come nearer. "Not because of the van," she said to Hookey, who now sat down again where he had been before, "but in case he hurts his teeth on it." She gave a sudden sharp look at him as she was about to turn back to the lookout tree. "Was it you—those punctures?"

Hookey grinned at her, which was a terrifying experience, like the coming to life of a gargoyle. "Roofing tacks. In me pocket from mending me net-shed roof."

Rissa grinned, too, widely and spreading. A quick glance at Tamzin who still tried to make peace with her dolphin, and then she was swinging up into the tree again. "Tamzin! The *Emma*! She's half-way here and coming a terrific pace."

"Pipe down!" Hookey snarled at her. "Want Barrett and them to hear you?"

Rissa glanced at him scornfully. "What does it matter? They'll see for themselves in a minute." Anything could happen now, with Jim and Roger and Meryon coming she was sure Jim would be with them. "They must have finished fishing early. The gods are with us!"

Tamzin didn't answer. She was too close to Simo and the whole thing was too tricky. She dared not do anything except talk softly to the dolphin. But she was listening, her heart racing with excitement at the thought of the *Emma's* dash to their rescue. Rissa's voice floated over the pool again.

"Someone riding out from Castle Farm. Mr. Merrow, I think. I suppose they're wondering what's happening. The *Emma's* gone straight through the gap in the fence they made for the van."

Tamzin put out a hand, but suddenly Simo wasn't there. The next second she was up again on Tamzin's other side. It was as if she must stay close, but couldn't bring herself to risk being touched again. She looked at Tamzin with her expressive and mobile eyes, moving her tailflukes very gently to remain where she was.

"The *Emma's* passed the van," Rissa called out, "but they've mended their wheel and they're putting the tyre back on. It is Mr. Merrow; he's on Patsy and cantering."

Patsy was the Castle Farm lookering pony, a looker being a shepherd in Sussex and Kent. Tamzin could visualise her homely bay figure sedately cantering nearer and thought of it as bringing one more rescuer: not that she could think of anything whatever that the old farmer could do, except possibly trouble Simo more. And Simo, it seemed, had lost confidence in the human race. But at least, Tamzin tried to console herself, if she, Simo's friend, could not get close enough to touch her, how much more difficult it would be for strangers.

The *Emma* swung round at the pool and stopped with a flourish that Meryon wouldn't have dreamed of in normal driving. Rissa was at the door as the boys and Jim got out. Meryon took in the existing situation in a couple of sweeping glances while Roger did the explaining, "Ran into a shoal and got all the fish we could carry; two boxes on board the *Emma* for Simo. They told us at the vicarage about this." He waved an arm. "Mr. Grey said if anyone had thought to ask him he'd have said who's got the fishing rights of the Redshanks' Pool."

Rissa gaped at this obvious wisdom which they had somehow completely overlooked. "Of course! No one can fish here who hasn't the fishing rights!"

"That goes for us, too, of course," Roger pointed out.

Rissa dismissed this. "Does that honestly bother you? How can it matter, as long as *they* can't?"

"Not that Simo is a fish, of course," said Meryon, "but the vicar says it means you can't fish, not even for old boots."

"We could stop them dead, absolutely!" Rissa exclaimed. "But who has the rights? Does anyone know?"

Everyone shook their heads, even Hookey who affected not to be listening but was doing so, most acutely.

"Mr. Merrow might know," Meryon said, watching the farmer's approach round the pool on Patsy. "He ought to; he rents the farm and the pool is on it, but Mr. Grey doesn't think he has the fishing rights. Tamzin having trouble with Simo?" She was swimming back now, the rope still coiled on her shoulder.

"She is that, and you can't wonder," the ferryman said. "Nor you can't. Dolphins is only human, arter all. What'd you do, mate, iffen your best friend took and flung you into a blessed dirty dungeon? Thass what this muddy ole puddle seem like, I'll lay, to a creature used to clean sea."

Uttering small interested whinnies towards Skylark and Cascade the bay lookering pony halted by the *Emma*.

"Having a picnic?" Mr. Merrow inquired with mild humour. He was old and grey but still powerful and tough. The hand on Patsy's rein was a key to its owner's character.

Everyone looked to Meryon to explain in a few clear words, and he did so; he was good at that. All Mr. Merrow's astonishment at the goings on, almost under his nose, was set aside in the obvious emergency. He said at once, simply, "Lord Trent is who has the rights, up at Ownsworth Hall. You know?"

The boys and Rissa gazed at each other, remembering a recent time when the Trent son and heir, the Honourable Aubrey, had joined them in holiday odd-jobbing.* It might or might not help their cause with the father, who did not see eye to eye with his son's political activities.

"He don't *do* any fishing here," Mr. Merrow said, "but he likes to have the rights, for to stop other people. It's in the view from his house, you unnerstand."

Meryon had been hauling out the boxes of fish. He swung round and slid into the driver's seat. "Anyone coming?"

Rissa hesitated, very torn, then said, "I oughtn't to leave Tamzin."

The ferryman also declined. "I had enough of ole *Emma* flogging me bottom over the Marsh. I lay I'm saddle-sore, fifty mile an hour across country at my time of life."

Roger leapt in and banged the door as Tamzin came up out of the pool, running with water. "Are you going, as soon as you've come?"

"We're on to something," Meryon told her. "Rissa'll tell you. I think it's going to be all right."

Hearing a roar behind them Rissa turned suddenly. "The van's on the move again! Hurry, oh hurry!"

"Back in ten minutes," said Meryon, slipping into gear. "Or thereabouts."

* Told in The Hoodwinkers.

CHAPTER XVIII

Something for his Lordship
to Sign

"REALISE what speed you're doing?" Roger said, trying to sound casual. The lane was both narrow and winding.

"Mm." It could have meant anything, but Roger had the impression it meant that Meryon neither knew nor minded much as long the hearse was doing the utmost possible in the circumstances. In fact, Meryon could see quite well over the hedges.

"Have to slow down a bit when we get to the corner," Roger suggested, his hands flat on the seat beside him. Telephone poles flew by, holiday people pressed themselves into the hedge and gaped, Roger and Meryon took off from their seats going over a humped bridge. Of the two steep hill-roads that go up into Winklesea Meryon chose the farther.

"One thing about these old hearses," he said, "they can't do much over sixty, but they do it just the same, hill or flat."

Roger clutched the door-handle as the *Emma* swung round the acute corner at the bottom of the hill and began to accelerate up it. "So they may, but don't you think it's a bit conspicuous in a thirty limit?"

"I don't really very much care." He was thinking of Tamzin swimming out to Simo again, while the big van from the aqua-circus unloaded its dolphin-catching equipment at the edge of the Redshanks' Pool. "As a matter of fact we've already had our number taken. Didn't you see the cop at the corner?"

"No; too busy looking at the corner." He drew in his breath sharply. "I'm sure you got that dog's tail."

"So, as we're copped already, we may as well make the most of it. Tail all right; I saw it in the mirror."

Four women talking at the roadside stared with open mouths and eyes.

"Bet they think it's some funeral," Roger said. Now that no caution could save them from the law he was beginning to enjoy himself. The *Emma* swept on through the quiet fringe of the ancient little town.

"Thinks she's going home," said Meryon, "but she's mistaken. Only hope Mother and Dad aren't looking out."

Swooping past his own gate and on down the road Meryon suddenly saw to his horror a flock of sheep come pouring out from a side lane just ahead of them. "Hold tight!" His two feet jammed down on the pedals. "Always wanted to try a real emergency stop," he said, the *Emma* bouncing to a standstill inches from the flock.

"High-speed non-turbulent braking—only not very," said Roger, rubbing his forehead: and then he saw something and inspiration flashed. "Just a minute; must have that." In a second, while sheep in their scores pressed bleating past the hearse, he had leapt out and over a gate and was running down the field.

"Hey, what the——?" Meryon had leaned across the seat and out of Roger's window. Roger was running very fast. There was a large pool at the bottom of the field. A tottery notice-board stood beside it. Meryon knew what it said:

PRIVATE. NO FISHING.

When Roger tore it from the ground he suddenly

understood. A grin spread broadly on his face as he jumped out and rushed round to open the coffin-doors. Roger came up panting, bearing the notice like a banner. He threw himself over the gate. "Something for His Lordship to sign!" he said, and slung it through the doors. "We can return it to-morrow."

Meryon slammed the doors. "Come on; we may have to drive fast, now, to make up for lost time."

Tamzin heard the news with hope rising again, but her eyes turned anxiously from Simo to the approaching van as she listened. "How long might they be, at the outside?

"You know the distance as well as any of us," Rissa said, "but none of us knows if the old chap is at home."

"And there's punctures," said Jim. "What can happen to Barrett can happen to us: *Emma* she always were a contrarious unseamanlike vessel."

"Depends who's at the helum," Hookey remarked.

"I'm going back to Simo." Tamzin was wading into the pool again, looking everywhere over it for the surfacing fin.

"Give us a hand pitching the fish in, Sunshine," Jim said to Hookey. "Be practice fer throwing in the circus blokes; and anyways no one can't catch an empty dolphin."

"Good reason fer not throwing 'em in, then, ent it?"

Jim thrust his little beard out. "She gotter get a rope on it, ent she? Well then. Come on, the enemy's snortin' in yer ear-'oles."

The old farmer had ridden on his rounds again, and Rissa had gone to calm Skylark at the noise of the van arriving. Small splashes of fish falling into the water were lost in the roar of the powerful engine drawing up in low gear.

The speed and assurance of action on the part of the

circus men took Rissa and the fishermen completely by surprise. Their plan must have been carefully worked out in advance to the minute and last detail. At once two of them were running out a dinghy with an outboard motor from the back of the van while the other two unloaded a rolled net. There was no standing on the bank and assessing the situation first. Mr. Barrett himself came over to Jim and Hookey, obviously intending to be apologetic and friendly. Tamzin saw all this in dismay and turned her back on it to concentrate completely on getting her rope round Simo. So it was that she didn't see at all what happened next.

"Sorry it had to come to this," Mr. Barrett was saying regretfully. "I really am. But I saw the lass was only playing for time, and in business time is what you haven't got. Still hoping she'll come round and join us when we've got the dolphin."

"You better lay off, mate," Jim said abruptly. "Private fishing. No one ent allowed."

Mr. Barrett looked around. "There's no notice."

"Notice be danged, I tellee it's private. Coupler chaps just gorn to git the cerstificate to prove it."

"Isn't Tamzin fishing in there, herself?"

"She didden know it were private. Now she do she ent fishing, see, just swimming around."

"It sounds a bit fishy to me," said Mr. Barrett, smiling at his pun. "You can't expect anyone, really, to take any notice of such a story? You're simply trying to hinder us. Well, I'm sorry, but we don't intend to be hindered."

The ferryman returned for his smile a glance like a sword as he strode past Mr. Barrett without a word, making for Skylark and the donkey-cart.

"He knows the van's near," Rissa said, passing Jim on her way back to the bank, "but I think he's all right; quite safely tied and facing the other way."

The ferryman nodded briefly, striding on. Hookey, incredibly enough, appeared to be helping with the launching of the circus dinghy. Rissa knew him well enough to know that he must have other motives; and sure enough, suddenly somebody tripped over something and two men were in the water. Some calculation must have gone wrong because one of them was Hookey, and Hookey, like most of the older fishermen, couldn't swim. The water was not deep near the bank but it shelved very suddenly. Rissa began running, but a noise of faster feet came up behind her. Turning as she ran she saw Skylark, his long ears back and tufted tail in the air, galloping with his teeth already bared towards the big van. His harness was still on him but unbuckled. Rissa looked from the donkey to Hookey but she only hesitated a moment. Hookey needed no help, the enemy were already hauling him out, but Rissa ran down to the water pretending she had never noticed Jim's flagrant act of sabotage.

It was not the first time Meryon had driven the old hearse up the long drive to Ownsworth Hall. In the days of the odd-jobbing enterprise it had once or twice stood in the great courtyard, next to the Honourable Aubrey's red Jaguar, looking rather like an elderly duchess chaperoning a dashing young debutante.

"Just like old times," said Roger, seeing the Jaguar there in its usual place. "Even the Hon. Aub with his head in the boot!"

The heir to Ownsworth looked up in astonishment as Meryon jumped out of the *Emma*. "Well, old boy, fancy you! How awfully nice to see you." He was about Meryon's age but as different as might be.

Meryon wasted no time. He was driven by the thought of the others at the pool, trying to hold off an enemy stronger both in men and equipment. "Hallo; father anywhere about? Sorry to be in such a rush but it's urgent."

"Well, actually, old chap, it's jolly awkward just now; he's interviewing another tutor for me. Not that I want one. Quite impossible to disturb him at the moment. But I've got to drive the fellow to catch his train in half an hour, so he can't be longer than that."

"Too late. Surely there's another train?"

The young man turned up his hands in despair. "Probably. But it's as much as my allowance is worth to go in there, now."

"Where? The library?"

"Oh, I say, old man——" Aubrey was horrified, perceiving Meryon's intention.

Meryon, however, knew from simple observation that the old lord had a weakness for Roger and himself, perhaps because he had always wanted a husky outdoor son as the heir to his estates, but instead had the elegant, politically misguided dilettante that was his impression of Aubrey.

"That's all right, I'll tell him you tried to stop me! Could be a matter of life and death——" Already he was half-way up the sweeping front steps, but suddenly he turned and dashed back to the hearse. Hauling out the notice-board from the back he tore up the steps again and vanished through the open front door.

Roger smiled at Aubrey with a helpless shrug. "I dare say I'd do more good staying here."

Tamzin heard the rending of Skylark's teeth and hoofs on the metal-work of the van and looked round knowing what she would see. Good old Jim! That would hold up the launching of the dinghy for at least a minute or two, until they caught and tied up the donkey. And two men in the water, too! There was some good work going on, somewhere, though she could see no sign of Jim or Hookey; only Rissa, knee-deep in the water helping—or could it be hindering?—the rescue. Tamzin began swimming away down the pool. If she couldn't catch Simo, at least she could draw her off as far from the launching place as possible, though still keeping the boat within sight.

Simo was as nervous as a wild pony about being touched, but as anxious to keep near Tamzin as a trained guard-dog. In a way, Tamzin was glad that she had not been able to get a rope on her. If the earlier capture had made Simo as wary and mistrustful as this, another determined attempt might alienate her for ever. If only, Tamzin grieved to herself, there were some language to communicate with animals! She had thought it before and surely would think it again, as people must who have to do things they would rather not, for an animal's own good. Now, if only the launching of the dinghy with its expert catchers could be delayed a little longer, it might never be necessary to break trust with Simo again, she thought; and then suddenly remembered—the day would still come when they would have to take her back to the sea.

Jim and Rissa had reckoned without Mr. Barrett himself. Although he had none of their and Tamzin's hatred of caging animals, he had a confident and capable way with them, and after his fashion he loved them. Now he ushered the dolphin-catchers back to their dinghy, including the one who was wet through, and said that he would deal with the donkey himself. He made no appeal for help to Rissa or to Hookey, who sat squeezing the water from his clothes, but walked straight up to the ravaging donkey and put out his hand.

"I hope he bites it," Rissa said to Hookey. But even that couldn't help much now. The dinghy was afloat, loaded with its net and equipment and crewed with its catchers.

In less time than Roger and the Honourable Aubrey could believe, Meryon came leaping down the wide steps. Both of them rather feared that he had been thrown out. Aubrey, in fact, was already saying, "Too bad, old man, too bad," as Meryon swung past him and into the hearse, sliding the notice in before him.

"Not at all," said Meryon, starting the engine. "Sorry there's no time to stop and tell you, just now."

Roger was tumbling in, grabbing for the door-handle, slamming it as the *Emma* started forward. The last they saw of Aubrey as they turned was his flopping dark hair above big dark eyes in an astonished face.

"Absolute stroke of luck," Meryon said as they swooped down the drive. "Told him where you got the notice from. Pool belongs to a farmer he can't stand, because he's put up concrete buildings in his view. Only too glad to sign it. Interested in the dolphin, too, and thinks the way we do about cages and tanks." He swung out on to the road and Roger grabbed at his open window to steady himself.

"Wasn't he furious—your rushing in?"

"No. Not when he saw it was urgent. A bit astonished. Nice old chap, really. Aubrey underestimates him. Keen on wild life, and says he's coming down to see Simo. Going to put up a proper notice, too. Says he kept meaning to, but the estate keeps him so busy."

Roger shut his eyes as they overtook a large pearl-grey saloon.

"It's all right," Meryon said reassuringly. "Can't be copped twice. And anyway," he added, "the only driving that's wrong is dangerous driving."

Roger looked at him.

"This isn't dangerous," Meryon explained, swirling round a bend, "only fast: because I know exactly what I'm doing. Just there, for instance, you could see clear round the corner, over the hedge. You don't think, do you, that I'd risk not getting back to them?"

In the ordinary way Meryon never drove the *Emma* fast. The astonishing thing to Roger was that he was so well able to do so when the need arose. After a minute he said, "What'd he sign the notice with?" He had been looking at it over his shoulder, the signature large, bold and bright red.

"Lady Mary's lipstick," Meryon said. "Pretty effective, isn't it?"

CHAPTER XIX

Escape from Captivity

TAMZIN had forgotten Simo's love of boats. The first splutter of the dinghy's outboard engine arrested the dolphin's interest. Hesitating, she turned with a flip of her tail and looked back, although Tamzin called to her with anxious urgency. For a minute, as the dinghy pushed nearer over the water, Simo glided backwards and forwards, trying to be in two places at once; but each glide went farther towards the dinghy.

"Simo! Simo!" Tamzin called from beyond the farther island; then suddenly in despair she put down her head and began swimming back fast towards the dolphin.

Simo was racing now with all her stream-lined speed, as if knowing Tamzin was following. She left Tamzin behind as a swift might leave a sparrow. A yard from the dinghy she demonstrated her powerful braking. Then suddenly diving she went under the boat and came up the other side, into the net that had been designed to catch her. It was over as quickly as that.

Tamzin felt as if her heart and her lungs were bursting as she flailed towards the dinghy, the one with despair and the other with an effort beyond her strength. There was hardly breath to cry out when she was near enough, "No! No! Don't take her! You can't, it's private fishing."

"Well, miss, we've got orders. Sorry. Your friends said the same about the fishing, but the boss says there's no authority."

Tamzin gripped the side of the dinghy, gasping painfully. "But there will be; someone's gone to get it. Oh, please let her go! She's my dolphin, everyone knows she's my dolphin."

The men were obviously sorry to distress her; but they had all they could give their minds to at the moment in securing the net round Simo for the tow to the shore. They were also, understandably, elated at the way the dolphin had played straight into their hands, when they were prepared for a long battle of wits and strategy. Finally they had everything in order and prepared to start towing.

"Sorry, miss, we really are; but dolphins are anybody's dolphins and you have been asked to come with her."

Grieving like a mourner, Tamzin swam after the dinghy and the captured dolphin as a mourner follows a bier. The outboard motor made too much noise for her to hear anything else, and she was too dulled by despair and exhaustion to notice Jim and Rissa dancing on the bank. But when the *Emma* bounced past the willows with a fanfare on her horn even the outboard couldn't smother the joyous sound, nor the battle-cry of Skylark's bray as he viewed the approach of another motor vehicle from his new tethering place, to say nothing of the ferryman's yells of triumph and encouragement. Cascade was whinnying, too, but quite unheard in the racket, as were Simo's small distress whistles.

Very puzzled, the crew of the dinghy nosed towards the bank where Mr. Barrett was awaiting them. They were not puzzled for long. Out from the hearse burst Roger and Meryon, carrying high between them the lipsticked notice. Rushing down the bank to shouts from Rissa and Jim and a joyful scowl from Hookey, they planted the notice squarely in the mud and shingle exactly where the dinghy was coming in. There it stood, solid, unarguable, totally forbidding:

PRIVATE. NO FISHING. By Order; TRENT.

"How's that, sir?" Jim shouted to Mr. Barrett, sticking his beard out.

The circus manager spread his hands. "We nearly beat you to it."

Meryon was stamping the damp earth round the notice-post. "And fishing means fishing for anything, even old boots, the vicar says," he explained, in case anyone held out that a dolphin wasn't a fish.

Mr. Barrett had many good points in his character, and one was a complete acceptance of the unavoidable. "Let her go," he said to the dinghy men.

Meryon suddenly had an idea. "Couldn't Tamzin let her go? It might, in a way, make up." She had reached the dinghy now and stood in the shallow water close to Simo.

Mr. Barrett didn't know what it might make up for, and he wasn't greatly interested. He had lost this round, if not the game. If the dolphin was to be freed it hardly mattered who freed her. "As you like," he said, and he glanced back at his tank-van already thinking ahead towards its next job.

Tamzin put out her hands to the net. "It's all right, Simo!"

The dolphin shot out from the opened meshes, straight and fast into the middle of the pool where she leapt high with a swirl of falling water. Tamzin watched her, shiny-eyed and silent; she had no words.

But Mr. Barrett had. Walking back up to the van he paused and looked over his shoulder. His attitude was still friendly; he had no wish to be at odds with these young people; but he was not prepared to be beaten by them. He said, "Of course this truce, or what you like to call

it, only applies while the dolphin's in the pool. You
realise that, don't you? Anyone can fish in the sea.'

Just then, in the triumph and relief of Simo's escape
from captivity, this seemed to be a trivial remark.
Sufficient unto the day, Tamzin thought; she's safe for
a long time yet.

We'll release her in the sea when the hullabaloo's died
down, Meryon thought; they can't sit around watching
all the summer; and there's hope of good news to-morrow
about the Order in Council.

Monday brought school as usual for all of them, and a
physics examination for Meryon; and, in the evening,
the disappointment of their hope. The vicar was called
to the telephone just before supper and came back with
the news to Tamzin and her mother in the kitchen.

"That was Charles Powell, the Member. It seems
awfully hard, but he says an Order in Council is out of the
question."

"Dad!"

"But why?" Mrs. Grey asked, pausing with the knives
she was counting on to the trolley. "They did it in New
Zealand; why not here?"

"Twice in New Zealand!" Tamzin said. She had been
washing lettuce and stood with wet hands, shocked and
incredulous.

"It's just that the laws of England and New Zealand
are different. You must have some existing legislation
on which to base an Order in Council, even in the Domin-
ions. Unfortunately, so Powell tells me, the only law of
that kind applying to British waters was established by
International Convention. And that means that to
invoke an Order in Council affecting Simo the Government would have to call an International Convention."

Tamzin and her mother looked at him in dismay. The
vicar didn't really need to add, "Obviously, as Powell

says, no government is going to do that for one dolphin, no matter how unusual."

"In any case," Tamzin said bleakly, "it would take far too long."

Mrs. Grey tried to see the best of the situation. "The way things have worked out, she may not need protection. It's wonderful about the fishing rights of the Redshanks' Pool. Richard, you were a genius to think of that."

"How long do you think she'll be safe there?" Tamzin asked. "Till the autumn, when dolphins migrate to warm waters?"

"It simply isn't possible to say, is it?" the vicar said. "After all, she's a sea animal, and the pool isn't the same as the sea. Dolphins have been kept in tanks and pools for quite long periods, even years, but the water is probably very carefully controlled. The trouble about the Redshanks' Pool is that it's almost static."

Jim had been out fishing that day and Tamzin had arranged to take two boxes of fish in the donkey-cart out to the pool, where she was to meet Meryon. Secrecy was not so urgent now that Mr. Barrett knew where Simo was, but still she hoped that the dolphin pilgrims would not find out too soon and crowd to the Redshanks' Pool. The morning papers were already speculating on the "shy dolphin of Westling; is it Simo?" "What has happened to Westling's Friendly Dolphin?" they asked, going on to report on the lonely far-out fin and the disappointed crowds who had braved the week-end weather to no avail. "Dolphin Girl not at Home. Vicar Says he has No Comment," said another paper. Not one of them seemed to have landed on the story of the Battle of the Redshanks' Pool, as Tamzin thought of it: she was glad about that.

Wondering how on earth they were ever going to be

able to pay Jim for all the fish he was supplying, she went round to Skylark's stable.

When she arrived at the pool it was about an hour to sunset. Meryon was there, his bicycle propped against a willow where so much had happened the day before. Tamzin knew at once from his sober face that something was not quite right. He said, "Hallo, I've only just got here; I haven't seen her yet."

Tamzin went to the edge of the bank still leading Skylark, not waiting to tie him up first, and looked over the water. The first thing she saw was a small fish floating belly-upwards; then another, and another. Meryon was holding her free hand. He had seen the fishes first; he knew what she would be thinking.

"They're dead," she said. "They must be the ones you brought for Simo in the *Emma*."

He nodded, hardly knowing what to say, too apprehensive himself of what floating fishes might mean. Tamzin was looking for a sign of Simo. She called her name anxiously, but no swift fin came racing through the water.

"If she was here, and all right, she'd have eaten the fish, wouldn't she?"

Meryon didn't believe that she was not there. "I'm certain Mr. Barrett wouldn't take her from the pool, now. Perhaps there was just more fish than she wanted."

Then they saw her; a slow dark shape in the dark water. She came up to breathe quite close by where they were standing. Her movements had lost their old snap and precision. Tamzin heard the clear "Ph-HOO-p" of her air-change, the only thing that still seemed like the old Simo. Thrusting the reins into Meryon's hand she ran, kicking her sandals off, and waded into the water. They were both wearing shorts, knowing that they might be wading. The joy of having Simo come nosing round her again, brushing her legs, was clouded by the knowledge that something must be wrong with her.

Meryon tied up Skylark and came into the shallow water. Simo let him rub her back, as she had always done. Tamzin looked up. "Is it because we're forgiven, or because she isn't well?"

"Because of both. We're going to have to move her," he said. "You know that."

She nodded.

"Better to take her chance in the sea," he went on, "than die in a pool that isn't right for her. It's too static, I expect. No real change of water, except through the shingle."

Simo stayed beside them, moving only a little. She seemed listless, a quality so unlike her that Tamzin's heart ached. She said to Meryon, "It'll be a very big chance that she takes. There's no hope of an Order in Council. We heard this evening."

"But she's got to take it, hasn't she? At least it will be a chance, which is more than I think she has here."

"Yes, she's got to take it, I know."

There seemed nothing else to say. It was a hard blow, after the glorious victory over the fishing rights. Now they were right back, facing the problem again; their high hopes over the Order in Council shattered, the freedom of the Redshanks' Pool no use.

Tamzin was thinking, Life's just a game of snakes and ladders; but she didn't say so, she didn't want to say anything.

Meryon said, "Well, I suppose we'd better throw in the fish we've brought. She might be tempted by fresh ones." He was thinking all the time about the best way and the best time to move her to the sea.

While they were throwing in the new fishes, which Simo idly pushed with her snout and nibbled at, they heard trotting hoofs and looked up to see Mr. Merrow riding round the pool on Patsy. He drew rein as he came near and called down to them.

"Piece of luck seeing you two. I just been riding along the foreshore looking for a couple of lost ewes. There's a dolphin stranded there, just below the lifeboat house. I called my dog off but there weren't much else I could do. Needs two people to lift one, say the least."

"Is it alive?" Tamzin asked quickly.

"And squeaking," said Mr. Merrow.

"It's her mate!" she said to Meryon, but of course he knew.

He thanked the farmer. "We'll go out there at once and see what we can do."

"That'll be dark afore long, son."

"There's a moon," Tamzin said, thrusting wet feet into her sandals, "and Skylark knows the way back. But even if there wasn't and he didn't, we'd go. Oh, I do hope he's still alive."

CHAPTER XX

Dolphin's Mate

SKYLARK was used to the ferryman's whirlwind driving. As a retired but still young, racing donkey he liked speed himself and needed little encouragement. It seemed, too, as if he were glad to get away from the Redshanks' Pool.

Tamzin said, leaning into the wind of their speed, "Of course Seaborn Sarah couldn't be walking now, on a night as calm as this; I expect he's just scaring himself, remembering her."

Meryon said nothing, wishing in his logical way that more could be known about spirits, if only enough to answer the basic question of whether they existed or not. To Tamzin their whole existence was logical enough to need no explanation; as, indeed, it seemed to be to Skylark. She didn't trouble to give it more thought, but pondered about the stranded dolphin.

"Do you suppose he was trying to reach Simo?"

"How could he know where Simo is?"

"You've only to think of moths," she said, "finding each other across miles."

The little cart bumped and rumbled and the black donkey galloped zestfully with his long ears pointed forward like lances.

"One donkey that would never need a carrot on a string in front of him," said Meryon, "but in his case, I suppose, it would have to be a model motor-car."

They rushed and bumped on in silence over the wide

green Marsh where the sky is half the landscape, until they reached the yellow ridges of the beach banks. Here they jumped out of the cart to help Skylark, Tamzin leading and Meryon pushing behind. The donkey's little hoofs sank nearly to the fetlocks in the shingle, but he pounded gamely on, dragging the crunching wheels behind him.

The tide was nearly as far out as it could get, and the evening chilly after the burning heat-wave. No people seemed to be about, even at the farther end of the beach where Simo usually came. Those who had been there had gone away early, disappointed in the non-appearance of their gay dolphin. Tamzin and Meryon didn't even glance along the shore, but straight ahead over the wet sand that was shining in the sunset. They saw the stranded dolphin at once, a long dark mound lying helpless where the shingle met the sand.

"Oh, no!" Tamzin exclaimed when she saw where it was. "Can we possibly carry him as far as that? He could hardly be much higher, or the tide lower."

"There isn't time to go for help," Meryon said. "Perhaps we can get him into the cart."

They took the downhill slope of pebbles to the sands in great sliding strides, their shoes leaving dents in the shingle beside the deep wheel-tracks. Skylark threw himself into his collar like a little plough-horse, sniffing the sea.

The dolphin was alive.

"But he's dry!" Tamzin cried in dismay. There was a tide-pool nearby, a mirror of red sunset. She whirled round looking into the cart for something to bale with.

"They don't keep balers in donkey-carts," Meryon said. He stood on one leg and tossed her one of his tennis shoes, taking the other himself. Leaving Skylark peering at the dolphin from a few yards distance they ran to the pool and baled water with the shoes. The water ran over the dolphin's back like oil over dried-out leather. It left the dark skin smooth and very shiny. They ran again and baled more, the dolphin's eyes following them. He was making the creaking noise that sometimes they had heard from Simo. It came from the blow-hole, they could see as well as hear. Often they had been so busy playing with Simo that they hadn't noticed where the sound came from.

Tamzin looked up questioningly at Meryon with the sodden shoe in her hand.

"The problem is, what to carry him on, if we can carry him," he said. "He's bigger than Simo, too big for the cart. We haven't got the rug and blanket."

Tamzin's seeking eyes rested on the black donkey. "There's Skylark's harness."

Meryon looked at it.

She said, "If we could get the girth under one end of him, and the breeching under the other, we might just manage."

Meryon was uneasy: even the tail end of this nine-foot dolphin would be heavy for Tamzin. He glanced at Skylark again, wondering how they might use his strength. It was a pity donkeys couldn't lift things. Now if Skylark had been an elephant. . . . Tamzin was running for another shoeful. Looking into the cart Meryon said, "There's the canvas Jim put over the fish-boxes. It's a bit small, but if we can lift him on to that perhaps Skylark could pull it, like a sledge."

Tamzin pounced on the idea. "We could make traces of the reins!" She always jumped at ideas when they seemed at all feasible.

They dragged out the canvas and inspected it.

"We're in luck; eyelet holes in the corners," Meryon said.

"I'll get the reins," said Tamzin.

Because they were donkey-sized reins they fitted through the eyelet holes. But for the same reason they might not be strong enough to take a big strain.

"They're all we've got," said Meryon, and Tamzin threaded them through and doubled and twisted them. They laid out the canvas on the sand close beside the dolphin. It was six feet by four: wide enough but too short; the tail end would have to hang over.

Skylark stood gazing out to sea, his ears idly flicking off flies. Anything could happen in his world and he took it all as a matter of course, unless it was frightening, or a mechanical monster that ought to be destroyed.

Meryon said, "See if you can link your hands under the tail end, and I'll try to lift the front."

Tamzin didn't believe he could, even just to the canvas; most of the dolphin's considerable weight was at the front and the skin was wet and slippery, now. When Meryon said, "Ready, lift!" it was all she could do to lift the tail end. Meryon's shoulder muscles showed under his white shirt as he took the strain of the fore-part. The dolphin began to squirm and struggle as soon as it was off the ground. Meryon's hands were sliding up under the flippers. He hadn't wanted to grasp the flippers in case of hurting the dolphin, but had to do so to avoid letting it fall too heavily. Warm breath, steamy from the blow-hole, puffed into his face. His own breath, pent with effort, blew back at the dolphin as they lowered it on to the canvas.

"We've done it!" Tamzin said exultantly. She stroked and patted the dolphin before dashing to fetch Skylark. "Really," she said honestly, leading up the donkey, "*you* did it. I knew you were strong, but I didn't know you were as strong as that."

He was bringing his shoes full of water from the pool

again. "Begorra, woman, you should see me playing cat's cradle with old railway lines."

She grinned, looking at him admiringly but briefly. They were both occupied now with linking the rein-traces to the harness.

They were surprised at the smoothness and success of the hauling plan. Skylark pulled away willingly, the dolphin scarcely struggled and there was no breakage of reins. Elation began to rise in Tamzin as they drew nearer to the sea, but Meryon knew that a game isn't over until the last whistle blows. With Tamzin leading him Skylark went into the shallow sea with no hesitation. Meryon was steadying the dolphin. It doesn't take much depth of water to float a dolphin, and soon Simo's mate was lifted by small lapping waves. The water was just above Tamzin's knees. She halted Skylark and turned eagerly to watch the return to the sea. Slowly the elation went from her as she saw, with dismay, the dolphin roll helplessly sideways, showing the light colour underneath.

Meryon stretched hands to right its balance, but the dolphin tilted back again after a second or two. It was obviously too weak from exhaustion to keep an even keel in the water; but this was vital if it were to be able to breathe.

"We'll just have to stay keeping him level until he can do it for himself," said Meryon.

Tamzin took Skylark back to the sand and tied him to the cart before running back to help. Together they helped and straightened the tired dolphin, guiding it about the shallow water like a model boat. The sun flared down behind Fairlight Cliffs in a blaze of red and the moon came up over the sand-dunes, cool and white. Still they guided the dolphin and still Skylark stood dozing, his head down, by his cart. It was nearly eleven o'clock when finally Tamzin and Meryon stood up straight and watched the dolphin swim away, strong and steady.

"Cold?" he said, taking her hand and rubbing it.

"Not really. At least, there wasn't time to notice."

Skylark had settled down on the sand when they came up to him, composed for the night with his legs folded underneath him. He looked up at them reproachfully and gave a long, sighing, toothy yawn.

"They'll be in a panic at home," Tamzin suddenly said. "Search-parties out and all, I shouldn't wonder. Oh, my poor parents! What they must suffer from me."

But as it happened, they hadn't. Mr. Merrow had bethought him of them, and had telephoned from the village to say that Tamzin and Meryon had gone on to the stranded dolphin. Mrs. Grey then telephoned Meryon's family, so that no one expected them home in any hurry. But when by half past ten they had not returned, Tamzin's parents decided there must have been trouble. The vicar, who had not ridden since his youth, saddled up Cascade, to that pony's astonishment, and rode out to see if he could help.

Skylark and Cascade knew of each other's approach through the night long before anyone else did, and set up an eerie exchange of brays and whinnies. They were answered by hair-trigger redshanks which always went up at the least disturbance. Tamzin thought it must be something to do with Seaborn Sarah again, in spite of the calm night and the moonwashed Marsh. By the Redshanks' Pool, where it was too dark to see Simo, she jumped with shock when she saw suddenly ahead of them a dark rider on a white horse. One hand tightened on the donkey's reins and the other went out to Meryon; but her father's familiar voice came shattering the bubble of her fear.

"Dad! I thought it was my last moment! And on Cascade!"

Because it was so late Meryon handed over the escort. He was invited to the vicarage for the night, but said he thought he ought to get back. He also said that he would take the canvas sheet with him as it had torn and needed repair. What he did not say was that he meant to get back to the beach, and that the canvas might be needed before morning. Picking up his bicycle at the Redshanks' Pool he rode home and found that his parents had gone to bed leaving a note and a tray of supper. He ate the supper, in company with the Burmese kitten who shared it, and left an answering note to his parents, knowing that both would understand. Then pulling on his thickest oiled-wool guernsey, he tied the rolled canvas to his bicycle with a length of good rope and rode back through the deserted darkness to the sea.

CHAPTER XXI

The Crisis and the Emergency

VERY EARLY the next morning Tamzin was awakened by three small pebbles thrown into her open north window. There was still an hour to sunrise and her room was dim with night. The first pebble dropped into a dream of dolphins and was Simo leaping in the sunlight. The second roused her, so that she lay half awake wondering what had awoken her. She heard the third one quite clearly falling "plop" on the polished boards, and jumped out of bed. Crossing the room to the window she trod on one; it hurt her bare feet and woke her up properly.

When she leaned out and peered into the dimness she saw a figure standing by the tennis court. Meryon's voice said quietly, "It's me. Can you come down?"

Tamzin felt a clutch of fear as she said, "Is it Simo?"

"No. Sh! Better not wake anyone."

"Coming."

She pulled jeans and a jersey on over her pyjamas and crept downstairs, thankful that the creaking stair had been mended. Twice, before, because of it, she had had to climb down the drainpipe to avoid disturbing her parents. It was dark for drainpipe climbing, now, in this hour before dawn.

In the garden the grass was wet with dew; her toes felt it. The trees were heavy black against a greying sky and the moon had gone. The whole village was quiet, even the cocks not yet crowing. Meryon took her hands; more than anything he hated distressing her.

She said, "You've been up all night."

He nodded. "I thought, if Simo's mate was trying to get to her, he might try again, and there'd be no one there."

"Did he?"

"Yes, twice."

"And you were there."

He said simply, "Yes," again: nothing of finding the dolphin at the tide's edge battered by inrolling breakers; nothing of his single-handed struggle to get it out to deeper water again, nor of the hours of watching and waiting on the dark lonely shore and the dolphin's second inrush when he was at his tiredest and coldest.

Tamzin guessed a lot of this.

He said, "It's high water now. I think too deep for him to strand himself easily. I took the chance to dash out, so that you'll know where I am. I'll be going straight back."

"I'm coming, too."

"No. You'll be more use organising things here: two dolphins in danger, now. Simo's got to be moved back this morning, to save them both."

"Then you're going to take something to eat."

He said, "As soon as it's light, go round and see Jim. Hookey, too. The more brains the better. Once Simo's back in the sea we've got Mr. Barrett to think of, again. D'you know if he's still in the village?"

She shook her head. "Jim will know."

"Get them out with the net and cart as quickly as you can. If I get a chance I'll go out to the pool and see if you need any help. But as long as the other dolphin keeps coming ashore I'll have to stay."

She nodded. "Wait while I get you something. There's a hunk of bacon-and-egg pie in the larder, and some fruit. I'll be quick."

Meryon came with her. "What I really am is thirsty." He drank at the cold tap, filling a beaker twice. Tamzin brought a bag, screwing the corners as she came.

"Ah, good!" he said. "Now I've had a drink I know I'm hungry, too. Must go, now. Will you give Mother a ring if you can, sometime? I left a note, but they'll be glad for more news."

"When you've had something to eat, you'll know you're tired."

"I know it now," he said, "but I haven't time to think of it." She felt her hands squeezed and he was gone.

Jim had always been an early riser, but when he went round to the ferry-hut in the milkiness of first-light he found Tamzin already there. Like Meryon, but without his absolute certainty of approval, she had left a note, hoping and trusting in her parents' continued understanding. It seemed better to her than arousing them so early.

"Jumping gin bottles!" said Jim, astonished. "You. And in the young of the day, gal."

"Yes; and I've got Skylark's harness on him, too. We must go quickly, Jim; it's urgent. Simo isn't well and her mate keeps casting himself ashore. Meryon's there; he's been there all night. Oh, Jim, I'm so worried."

Jim was simply splendid. At any other time he might have argued; he loved arguing; but now he saw the crisis and the emergency. "I'll goo fetch Hookey, mate. He's a unaccountable miserable sinner, but we gotter have him."

Relief surged over Tamzin. "We'll both go. Pull the cart out, Jim, and I'll get Skylark." They were hurrying to the stable. "I've stowed the net and the blankets and the petrol-tins."

Hookey was in bed and had to be got out. No banging on the door was effective, not even with Hookey's woolly dog barking as well; so Jim climbed in at a forgotten window and heaved him out, no matter that Mrs. Galley was there as well. Waiting outside holding Skylark, Tamzin heard a great deal of lurid language. She didn't take much notice; she had been used to fishermen's language since first she toddled round to the harbour. It wasn't allowed at the vicarage but was accepted as quite normal in the fishermen. Presently a noise of thumping feet came from the steep stairs and a minute later Jim and Hookey appeared round the corner of the house to a renewed frenzy of barking. Mrs. Galley slammed the bedroom window to shut out the noise and presumably returned to bury her ears in bed.

The donkey-cart seat really only held two. Hookey was bundled unceremoniously into the back, with the petrol-tins and blankets, in which he immediately composed himself to sleep again. Jim looked round at him as they set off down the road and said wickedly, "I lay us'll gallop when we gits to the bumps; that'll rattle 'im smartish, hey?"

Jim himself was driving. He was a much more furious driver than Tamzin was, because she couldn't help always considering the animal she was driving. To-day she knew that they must go fast, and preferred that anyone but she should be responsible. There was no doubt that Jim's driving rattled Hookey smartish. Fresh examples of sea-faring language mixed with a clatter of petrol-tins came to their ears, above the noise of wheels and hoofs and a kind of high yodelling from Jim that was meant to spur on the donkey.

Morning was coming to the Marsh in a flush of rosy mist. The lion-brown grazings, revived by the thunder torrents, were already greening to their usual lushness. Sheep rushed from the path like hens and stood watching their wild progress from safe places. Tamzin heard the redshanks go up, and knew that in a moment or two she would know if Simo was alive.

Meryon was at the Redshanks' Pool. He must have been there some time for the birds to have settled again. Sky-lark stopped in a series of stiff-legged jumps as Meryon came up. Tamzin could hardly bear the minute between seeing him and knowing his news. Anything could have happened to either dolphin.

He said at once, looking at her, "Both well—or as well as we can expect. I've just seen Simo. She's still pretty sluggish but I don't think much worse."

Relief once more surged in Tamzin. Always, these days, she seemed to be overwhelmed by anxiety or relief; life seemed to be an endless crisis. Hurrying again, she was tying up Skylark while Hookey and Jim unloaded their gear.

Meryon went on, "Remember that rather nice family staying at the Watch Houses? Little girls called Mary and Susan. Their father came down for an early swim before the tide got too low; most interested, said he'd keep an eye on the dolphin while I came out here. He knows what to do."

Tamzin had her swim-suit on as usual under her jersey and jeans and now was stepping out of these. "Jim says Mr. Barrett went away last night, but he hasn't cancelled his room at the Conqueror. He might be back any time, perhaps to-day, Mrs. Gudgeon told him. I said how Simo would be in awful danger again in the sea, and that we *must* think of something. Jim muttered and mumbled and said the best thing was to hang Mr. B. from the yard-arm; and Hookey never said anything at all."

"You can take heart from that, anyway: it's always a good sign when Hookey says nothing at all. It's when he talks that you can give up hope."

Tamzin glanced over her shoulder to see if Hookey

heard, but the men were at the water's edge soaking the blankets and filling up the tins.

The water was very cold under the mist, though the sun was drilling its way through and had already turned the mist to a golden haze. Taking the small rolled net under her arm Tamzin waded into the water, calling Simo. Her shivering went into her voice, so that it reminded Meryon of the redshanks. He, too, went into the water, but Hookey and Jim with the donkey-cart stayed ready and waiting on the bank, peering sharply into the mist.

Tamzin saw a dead fish floating, and a white swan's feather upcurled like a little gondola; and then Simo was there, rubbing against her legs and whooshing air.

"Slip the net under her," Meryon said. "I'll take the other side."

Almost, Tamzin felt like Judas as she leaned, patting her dolphin and sliding the net to catch her once again. But it was for Simo's sake. As the net closed round her, Meryon's hands securing it, Simo didn't struggle but lay quiet in the water.

"It's because she isn't well enough," Tamzin said, full of pity, but Meryon was already throwing the coiled line ashore for Jim and Hookey to haul in.

"You couldn't have had it easier," he said. "She'll be all right once she gets back to the sea."

"With Mr. Barrett on her trail again?"

"We'll think about Mr. Barrett," he said, "when we've got her into the sea."

CHAPTER XXII

The Most Important Thing

FOR THESE now practised dolphin-catchers and trans-porters, the next stage was easy. As they took the familiar trail, but this time in reverse, morning blazed on to the Marsh. Everything was in reverse this time, Tamzin reflected, walking at Skylark's bridle. Instead of darkness and the fiercest storm she could remember, there was this golden trumpet-blast of a July morning. Instead of flight from the sea there was a return to it—but it was, too, a return to danger.

Meryon ran ahead to relieve Mary's and Susan's father, who, setting out for a quick dawn swim, had already spent two hours in and by the sea. With Jim and Hookey supporting the dolphin's overhanging tail, there was only Tamzin to attend to the dousing. At regular intervals, now that the storm-torrents were not doing it for her, she called a halt to pour water over Simo's skin from one of the tins. The water just lasted.

Meryon had taken over from the children's father when the donkey-cart crunched across the beach banks. The tide was at the half, and he stood at the edge of it, barefooted. Just beyond him Tamzin saw at once the dolphin slowly cruising, back and forth. There was, obviously, an uneasy truce between the boy and the dolphin. Meryon glanced over his shoulder but did not come to meet the cart. As Tamzin led Skylark on over the hard wet sand she realised suddenly that both the dolphins were whistling.

"Do you hear?" she cried to Meryon excitedly. "They're calling to each other."

He nodded. "Talk about dolphin intelligence; this one knows I'm here to stop him coming ashore. He's simply waiting for me to go."

Full of exhilaration Tamzin said, "He won't wait much longer. Oh, look at him, fairly racing up and down!"

Practised now in these sea adventures, the donkey nonchalantly waded in, pulling his cart with its cargo over which so much anxiety and strife had been stirred. The noises of the dolphins filled the air now above the gentle splash of ebbing wavelets. With all their range of whistles and crackles and creaking sounds they called to each other in a kind of excitement that was infectious to the human helpers. One danger to Simo was for the moment forgotten in the exultation of having so nearly overcome another.

Skylark nosed the water and snorted into it while Hookey and Jim and Tamzin and Meryon took the corners of the under blanket, as they had done before, and lifted Simo down into the sea. Now the excitement of the lonely mate became a joyful madness. Like a little speedboat he streaked up and down in short bursts, making the baffling instantaneous stop at each turn. Simo drifted free from the blanket, slowly and cautiously at first, rocking with the rocking of the waves. The other dolphin raced round her, leaped over her, dived under her. Even the black donkey lifted his wet muzzle and watched; but the four helpers stood in the water entranced, Hookey as much as any of the others. He loved dolphins; they were perhaps the only things that he did love in the world of bitterness that he had created for himself. But he never spoke about this, nor of the reason for it.

Gradually at first, and then more and more dashingly,

Simo joined in what Tamzin always remembered as the dance of the dolphins.

"She's all right! She's really all right, not ill at all!" she said, thrilled and incredulous. Simo had seemed so listless in the Redshanks' Pool.

"I lay she were pining, gal," said old Jim. "Come on ashore, mates, 'r else us'll all have galloping rheumatitis."

One of the things that Tamzin had asked in the note she left for her parents was that Rissa and Roger might be telephoned as soon as possible. They arrived within ten minutes of each other, first Roger on his bicycle and then Rissa on Siani; she had left her bicycle at Castle Farm. Skylark and Siani stood glaring at each other and making provocative little squeals; but the six people, young, old and middle-aged, sat in a row on the shingle, silent as they stared at the dolphins. Tamzin couldn't have said a word if she had tried to; her mind and heart were too full. All she could do was look at the dolphins; and they leaped in the sunlight, like the dolphins in her dream, with silver water falling from them. She had in her pocket the little dolphin Meryon had carved for her and her hand closed round it.

Old Jim suddenly said, "I lay we gotter do something about that Barrett. Best thing'd be keelhauling."

"Oh, nonsense, Jim," said Rissa, "this isn't the seventeenth century. We must think of something we can *do*."

"Surely there must be someone else we can interest in the dolphins," Roger said, "besides the Government, who aren't?"

"But it's got to be now—to-day!" Tamzin exclaimed.

Hookey had been drying his nobbly feet with what might have been a handkerchief. He said, in his usual harsh and disagreeable voice, "They don't like drunks in the Royal Navy."

Meryon looked at him. "No, I don't believe they do."

After a moment of deep thought, still dabbing with his dark-grey rag, Hookey added to this, "Wuz in the Navy meself, once, time I were young."

There was a further pause in which everyone looked at him.

"'Course it's worse fer officers. Wuz a young 'un in my ship drank a bottle of Jamaica rum when we was put-in there. Fellers kidded him it were a local soft drink. That felled him like a pole-axed ox. But first he makes up to all the girls, and then he bashes up all the fellers, and next he bashes up the town. Funny thing, next morning the cap'n thought as it were me. I never said nothen; that made no difference to me. But it would've been the end fer an officer."

"Wasn't it the end for you, too, Hookey?" Rissa asked.

"I quit the Navy," Hookey admitted, "but took up fishing."

"Well?" asked Meryon, seeing that something must be leading up to something.

"That chap," said Hookey, "he's a cap'n hisself, now. Portsmouth. In charge of the Dolphin Experiment Station."

"We read about that!" Roger exclaimed. "It's all very secret, and they're studying dolphins' sonar, and the sudden stop, to see what can be learned for submarines."

"I don't want anyone to experiment on Simo!" Tamzin said. "It'd be worse than the aqua-circus."

"Hookey," said Meryon, "do you think you still have any, er, influence over this naval officer?"

Hookey studied his bare feet, stuck out in front of him. "He say, if ever there come a time——"

"And has there ever come a time?"

"I never seed him since."

Suddenly Meryon was on his feet, hustling Hookey on to his. "Quick, then! Give a hand, Jim. There isn't a moment to lose. Into the donkey-cart, Hookey. Never mind my bike. How far's Portsmouth? The *Emma*'s full of petrol, luckily. That's the idea, into the front." Everyone was pushing and hustling Hookey up into the cart. "No room for anyone else. Never mind, we'll be back as soon as we possibly can. Keep Barrett off the water until then, however you have to do it."

"Hey! What about my donkey-cart?" cried Jim as Meryon shook the reins.

"They'll be all right at my place until we get back." Meryon told him. He turned to look back reassuringly at Tamzin. "No one's going to take Simo from the bay." A little slowly over the beach, though with willing hands shoving behind, then as fast as only a racing-donkey can go, the little cart whirled away over the Marsh.

For one long nightmare day the others waited for their return. First there was the long trudge back to Westling, for which Jim was offered Siani but with dignity refused. There was the shock of seeing a small crowd already trekking out towards the Redshanks' Pool.

"How news gets around," said Rissa; "but luckily usually a day late. We don't mind them there, now."

There was the news from Mrs. Gudgeon at the Conqueror that Mr. Barrett was returning that afternoon. There was the news in the newspapers, hot on the trail now of Simo's secret removal. Two reporters were waiting at the vicarage gate, but Tamzin dared not tell them anything at all. How could one possibly know what was happening or what was likely to happen, or what news might further endanger the dolphins? She was afraid to go out to the shore again, now that the crowd had got hold of the idea that Simo was in the Redshanks Pool. Time had never seemed so endless nor so sinister with danger.

Mrs. Grey insisted on a belated breakfast for everyone, including Jim. There was some comfort for Tamzin in telling her parents all about the night's and day's events, while Diccon wandered about with tweezers catching midges for his sundews and saying that really he thought they were more interesting, and much less worrying, than dolphins.

Old Jim went round to the Point, brewing dark and fearful ideas designed to outwit Mr. Barrett and cripple his vehicles, and sat by his ferry-hut keeping his eye on the Conqueror. But Tamzin and Rissa and Roger decided that the only way things could be bearable would be by somehow keeping an eye on everything at once. Accordingly, on two ponies and a bicycle, they rode out to Cloudesley Castle, in the centre of their western stretch of marsh, and climbed the ruined seaward wall, their old lookout on many occasions. From here, high above the sheep and the fences and the dykes and widespread grazings, they could see nearly all the western Marsh, including the roads down to Westling and to Castle Farm. They ought to be able to see both Mr. Barrett's return to the village and the *Emma*'s approach to the sea. They could see the Redshanks' Pool with its growing crowd of sightseers driving the swans and the redshanks far away. In the distance a dark rim on the sea wall was the usual trail of Simo's pilgrims. The only thing they could not see was Simo herself. The sea, indeed, lay sparkling under the midday sun, a long shining ribbon of it in front of their eyes; but the inshore regions where the dolphins played were hidden from them behind the beach banks.

The ponies grazed the short grass that lay like a carpet within the castle walls; Roger's bicycle glinted under an elder tree and the three riders crouched up on the wall-top, watching in the sun.

At about half past two a vehicle came into view behind the willow trees on the track to Castle Farm.

"The *Emma*! There she is!" Tamzin cried. She jumped to her feet and stood gazing, waiting only to be absolutely certain before leaping down the grassy slopes to the ponies.

Rissa was never a victim of wishful thinking. One penetrating glance was enough. "It isn't the *Emma*. And if you aren't more careful you'll fall off the wall and give us all endless trouble getting you to hospital or something, at the worst possible time."

Tamzin's heart sank back into the doldrums as she saw that Rissa was right but it was thumping in excitement of a different kind when she recognised what the vehicle was. "It's the Aqua-circus van! Coming through the farm way, not Westling at all."

"Good grief!" said Roger. "And old Jim waiting to scuttle it at the harbour."

"Who would have thought——" began Rissa; but already they were scrambling and leaping down to the ponies and bicycle.

The van was at the sea before them; that is to say, as near as it could get to the sea. It was halted by the ramparts of the beach banks; but Mr. Barrett and his dolphin-catchers had walked on over the shingle to see what they could see. They didn't see anything at all of Simo, or her mate.

When they had tied the ponies at the lifeboat house, Tamzin and Rissa and Roger pounded up over the pebbles. They stood a little apart and gazed, too, over the calm sea. The water glimmered and rippled under a sun growing hot as before the thunder. Its surface was unbroken, except by fishing seagulls.

"She isn't there," Tamzin said hopefully, panting from the gallop and the run. "If only she stays away until the *Emma* comes."

Mr. Barrett's party stood looking and talking for a minute and then went back to the van. The sound of its engine came on the wind, nearer and nearer, and presently the van itself came into view above the highest ridge of shingle.

"Look at them," said Roger. "They're laying tracks. Two sets of planks; they lift them from the back wheels as they go over and lay them at the front again. That way they can get along quite fast."

"They think of everything," Tamzin said bitterly.

"That's elementary," said Roger.

"What can have happened to the *Emma*?" she cried.

"Could be at the beach banks," Rissa said. "From here we'd never know."

Tamzin looked at her with a sudden wild hope, and turned and ran back up the shingle. The *Emma* was there. She had just pulled up where the van had first been halted. Meryon and Hookey were tumbling out of the front. Someone else was with them, too. Tamzin gazed again, wild with excitement and suspense. Yes, it was— a naval officer. It must be Hookey's midshipman, whose drunken rampage Hookey had taken on himself. "But it can't be," she said to Roger and Rissa, who came up seeing her staring there. "Look at him; he could never have bashed up a town, even after a bottle of Jamaica rum."

"He was quite young, then," Rissa said. "He's just grown old and respectable, that's all."

"Everyone doesn't," Roger said as they ran towards the *Emma*. "Jim and Hookey haven't. And I never shall. Not respectable, I mean."

Meryon made swift introductions as they met, and

added; "It's all right! Captain Beamish will tell you."

The captain looked so distinguished that it was impossible to connect him with Hookey's rum-riot story. Hookey himself, standing near, looked like a barbarian beside a noble lord. But the captain was perfectly natural. He said, "I think your dolphin will be of the greatest interest to us. I hear she has been demonstrating their instantaneous stop. There are obvious difficulties in getting captive dolphins to do this. Perhaps if we could study a dolphin which will do it, here where she feels at home, we should learn quite a lot."

Tamzin's eyes widened and shone. "And not try to take her away?"

"Of course not. That would only defeat our purpose." He glanced back towards the hearse. "I had a notice drafted out before we left. It provides for the protecting of all dolphins within this bay, in the interests of National Defence, and until further notice. It's in your, er, estate car."

"I'll get it, sir," said Hookey with astonishing respectfulness and springing to attention; and he did so. The others began walking towards the lifeboat house. Hookey raced after them, as respectfully as a man can race, carrying a brief-case. The Aqua-circus van was now close down to the water.

"They have an outboard dinghy in that," Roger told the captain.

"No matter," said Captain Beamish. "Now, I think the door of the lifeboat house will suit our purpose admirably."

Hookey held up the brief-case like a silver salver while the captain opened it and extracted the notice.

"I have also a pot of paste," said the captain.

"I'll do it, sir," said Meryon, taking the pot.

The others watched, breathless and nearly heart-beat-less, while Meryon pasted up the notice. There it was by order of Captain Beamish, R.N. All dolphins in the bay. Tamzin gazed at it. The incredible, the impossible, the wonderful had happened.

"Of course, it's only a temporary protection," said the captain, standing back to survey it, "until I get full authority through from the Admiralty; but I think it's the only course I can take, in this situation and on the spur of the moment. In any case, it will protect the dolphin. Perhaps," he said, glancing down the beach, "I ought to go and have a word with this Mr. Barrett. He seems a very persistent person."

As soon as he had turned his back, Tamzin, Rissa, Roger, Meryon and Hookey suddenly linked arms, as by a kind of herd instinct, and began wildly but silently dancing in a circle below the notice.

"What Jim is missing!" said Rissa.

"Where's Simo?" Meryon asked as they stopped as suddenly.

"We haven't seen either of them," Roger said.

Everyone looked out at the sea, but there was no fin and no leaping dolphin.

"I think she's gone," Tamzin said. "I think they've both gone." She felt she knew.

"Nonsense," said Rissa, "they'll be back in the morning, you'll see. And under the protection of the Royal Navy. Look at Mr. Barrett stopping his men."

"But supposing they don't come back," said Roger, "what about Captain Beamish?"

Meryon said, "No one will have lost anything, except Tamzin and Simo, perhaps. But I think she'll come back; if not this summer, next."

"If they've gone," Tamzin said, "I mean gone for ever, I'll never know why. But I suppose it could be that she thinks I failed her."

"A dolphin got more sense than that," said Hookey with his unexplained absolute certainty.

"As long," said Meryon, "as you don't think she failed you. That's the most important thing. It wouldn't be like you to bear a grudge." But when he looked at her he knew that the important thing was safe, as well as the dolphins.